CURRY

**Center Point
Large Print**

**This Large Print Book carries the
Seal of Approval of N.A.V.H.**

CURRY

A WESTERN TRIO

MAX BRAND®

CENTER POINT PUBLISHING
THORNDIKE, MAINE

This Circle V Western is published by
Center Point Large Print in 2009
in cooperation with Golden West Literary Agency.

First Edition April 2009

ISBN: 978-1-60285-402-4

Library of Congress Cataloging-in-Publication Data

Brand, Max, 1892-1944.
Curry : a western trio / Max Brand. — 1st ed.
    p. cm.
ISBN 978-1-60285-402-4 (library binding : alk. paper)
1. Western stories. 2. Large type books.
    I. Brand, Max, 1892–1944. Jim Curry's compromise.
    II. Brand, Max, 1892–1944. Jim Curry's test.
    III. Brand, Max, 1892–1944. Jim Curry's sacrifice. IV. Title.
PS3511.A87C87 2009
813'.52—dc22
2009000043

CURRY

Acknowledgments

"Jim Curry's Compromise" by Max Brand first appeared in Street & Smith's *Western Story Magazine* (4/1/22). Copyright © 1922 by Street & Smith Publications, Inc. Copyright © renewed 1950 by Dorothy Faust. Copyright © 2009 by Golden West Literary Agency for restored material.

"Jim Curry's Test" by Max Brand first appeared in Street & Smith's *Western Story Magazine* (4/22/22). Copyright © 1922 by Street & Smith Publications, Inc. Copyright © renewed 1950 by Dorothy Faust. Copyright © 2009 by Golden West Literary Agency for restored material.

"Jim Curry's Sacrifice" by Max Brand first appeared in Street & Smith's *Western Story Magazine* (5/20/22). Copyright © 1922 by Street & Smith Publications, Inc. Copyright © renewed 1950 by Dorothy Faust. Copyright © 2009 by Golden West Literary Agency for restored material.

TABLE OF CONTENTS

EDITOR'S NOTE

Frederick Faust's most prolific year was 1922, in which his output consisted of eleven serials and thirty short novels, or the equivalent of twenty novels. The majority were Westerns published in Street & Smith's *Western Story Magazine*, his most important market from 1920 through 1933. The three short novels about Jim Curry in this volume appeared in that magazine in that year. Although Faust commonly featured series characters in his stories—Bull Hunter, Ronicky Doone, James Geraldi, Chip, Speedy, Reata, and Silvertip—Jim Curry is the most moving and tragic of these creations, since he is set on a course from which he can never return to a normal life when his father is wrongfully killed by a posse of masked men. As in THE QUEST OF LEE GARRISON (Circle Ⓥ Westerns, 1998), a Max Brand story can defy all generic conventions.

JIM CURRY'S COMPROMISE

I

Everyone was so used to seeing Jim Curry breezing and blustering about the town, hearing his great voice raised in laughter or in anger that the pale-faced giant who strode into the sheriff's office brought Sheriff Mason himself straight out of his chair.

"He's dead," declared Jim Curry. "He's dead. I dunno how it happened. He's dead!"

Curry stared at the sheriff, and Sheriff Mason stared at him. At last, thought the sheriff, Jim Curry had come to grief. Everyone had known that sooner or later the blow must fall. Always fighting, always ready for trouble, big or little, Curry had stormed his way through many years of life in safety, but the period of safety was approaching an end, so the sheriff felt, and so the whole town shared his feeling.

Curry was one of those fellows who never grew up. Marriage and fatherhood had not aged him. He wore long mustaches, and the holster of his revolver was worn thin, but inside their wrinkles his eyes were as bright and careless a blue as they had been in his youth. Women in the town had shaken their heads, when he was a youngster, and prophesied that "Jimmie Curry won't come to no good unless he settles down *pronto.*" That prophecy always hung like a heavy cloud over Curry. In fact, the whole community was waiting for the time when Jim Curry would take a step too far, a step from which he could not redeem himself through the simple expedient of a laugh and a smile. When he married and settled down on the little ranch, half a dozen miles from town, some people had a hope that Jim would give up his foolish way of life, particularly after Jim, Jr. was born. But there was no changing Curry. If he altered a little at first, after the death of his wife, he reverted to his old habits. The boy was allowed to raise himself. Jim Curry could not bother himself with such a problem as the rearing of a freckle-faced child. The child grew to be a man, and his father was past forty-five years of age. But the badge of his age was his mustaches and his wrinkles—his soul was as young as ever.

There was this difference as time rolled on. People forgive many things in a youth that are intolerable in a man. What had caused the citizens of Chester to smile when Jim Curry was twenty, made them shake their heads when he was thirty, and it made them scowl when he was forty. The world seems to have a certain limited stock of tolerance for pranks. Once the stock is exhausted, it goes hard with those who still make demands in the same direction. So it was with Jim Curry. He avoided one thing only. He was never contemptible. Those who were occasionally tempted to sneer at his antics revised their opinion when they considered the weight of his fists and his acknowledged skill with a revolver. In the use of the latter weapon, at least, Jim Curry had practiced industriously. But, in spite of all that was held against Curry, everyone really wished him well and the sheriff shook his head with a sigh when he started from his chair and heard that exclamation: "I dunno how it happened. He's dead!"

"Who's dead?" asked the sheriff. "Who've you run into this time, and who've you finished up?"

"It's . . . it's Jackson . . . it's Dad Jackson," replied Jim Curry.

The sheriff winced and changed color. This was quite another tale. "Jim," he said, "tell me that you don't mean it. Tell me that it ain't so."

For Dad Jackson, as he was fondly known, was the best-loved citizen of Chester. In the old days, Dad Jackson had been a very prosperous prospector, but his nearest and dearest friend, using his hold on the affections of Jackson to betray him, had nearly stripped him of his money. The blow had not robbed Dad Jackson of his trust in human nature, however, and there was hardly a man in Chester who, at one time or another, had not gone to Dad Jackson for help. Therefore it was that the sheriff winced, as if he

15

had been struck in the face, when he heard the fatality named.

"If unsaying it would undo it," declared Curry, "I'd sure unsay it. But unsaying it won't help. I seen him fall. I listened over him for his heart. He's dead, Sheriff, and he'll haunt me."

"Dead!" exclaimed Mason, and then he shrugged his shoulders and gave his entire body a vigorous shake to get rid of the inertia that the word brought to him. "Tell me the straight of it, Jim. What happened?"

"We were talking along friendly," said Jim Curry. "We were talking about some of the old times, and, in the midst of things, I started showing Mason the double roll, and a gun went off . . . and . . . ." He paused, unable to finish the description. "You come along with me, Mason and I'll show you. I . . . I can't no way talk about it as easy as showing you what happened out at Dad's house."

The sheriff nodded. "I'm plumb sorry, Jim," he said, "that this here happened. But I can't take you out there. You'll have to wait here until I come back." He opened a drawer in his desk and took from it a bunch of keys.

"Wait!" exclaimed Curry. "You don't mean that you'd lock me up, Sheriff?"

"It don't mean nothing, Jim," Mason assured him mildly. "It don't mean a thing. You just stay here, safe and quiet. Even if worse come to the

16

worst, which it won't, they can't do no more'n send you up for manslaughter."

"Send me up? Prison, you mean, Sheriff?"

"In a manner of speaking," said Mason not too adroitly, dodging the issue. "That's what I mean. You ain't going to die just because you stay overnight in jail."

But big Jim Curry was gray with fear of which the sheriff was not an altogether unknowing witness. He had seen, before this, big men and brave men tremble at the thought of imprisonment, men who would dare a hundred dangers readily enough in the open, but whom the thought of prison walls threw at once into a panic.

"Wait a minute, Mason," protested Curry, backing toward the door. "I come in here to tell you what's happened. I didn't come in to see you shove me into a cell and turn the key. Is that friendly, Mason? Or d'you think I'm so dog-gone' cheap that I'd let you do all of that without a fight?"

The sheriff nodded. "I know how you feel, partner. I'd like to let you out of this if I could, but it wouldn't be right, and it wouldn't be good even for you, Jim. You know how Dad Jackson stood with the boys around here. We all plumb loved that old man, Jim, and the boys are sure going to take it mighty hard when they hear what's happened. Just for a day or two, mind you, some of the gents are apt to talk about guns

17

and ropes and what not, and the best thing you can do, to keep your hide safe, is to get inside of steel bars and stay there. Understand?"

Jim Curry was still gray, and he shook his head. "I don't like it, Sheriff," he kept saying. "It makes me all wrinkle up inside. Takes all the starch out of me, you see?"

"I can't stand here arguing!" exclaimed the sheriff. "You step over here and go through that door, Curry. They's nobody else inside. You'll have the whole place to yourself . . . all the blankets you want for your bunk, magazines to read, and everything else. But inside you go. It's for the sake of your own neck that I'm talking, you fool."

As he spoke in this burst of temper, he walked across the room, straight at Jim Curry. And, quite unconsciously, he dropped his right hand on the butt of his revolver. It was a most unfortunate move.

On the very verge of being persuaded, Curry saw the sheriff apparently resort to the most violent of threats. Was it as serious a matter as that? He peered through the open door. The room beyond, used as a jail, loomed dark and forbidding to Jim. With all his soul he loathed that room.

"Mason," he pleaded, "don't push me too hard!"

"Why, you're a fool!" exclaimed Mason. "I

can't stay here all day and argue with you. Will you come along or do I have to call Harry and bring him in to help me drag you in there?"

Plainly the sheriff was very angry indeed, or he would never have suggested "dragging" to such a man as big Jim Curry. The answer of the latter was brief. It was not even as extended as a syllable. He found himself hemmed against the wall with no escape except by the use of force. And force, accordingly, he used. He stepped neither forward nor back, but, swaying a little to the left, he jerked up his right fist and landed it squarely under the chin of the surprised sheriff.

There was not a sound of protest. Only the head of the sheriff, as he fell, bumped loudly against the desk, and then he slumped to the floor, the rattle of his revolver muffled in the holster at his side.

Jim Curry looked down in relief. This obstacle was out of the way. That it might be replaced by another more formidable did not occur to him. Jim looked only from step to step in this future. He lingered, however, regardless of what danger might come to him from the sheriff's boy, Harry, in the next room. He lingered long enough to bend over the sheriff and make sure that he was not badly hurt. He had always been afraid to use his full strength on any man, but now, in the excitement of the moment, he had smashed up with all of his might.

Observing that the sheriff's jaw sagged crookedly to one side, he took hold of the end of it and stirred it. He could hear the scraping of bone on bone. Plainly that jaw was broken, badly broken. Moreover, at the back of the head appeared a gash, and under the gash was a growing pool of crimson. That was the result of the blow against the edge of the desk. Sudden panic rushed through the brain of the big man at the sight. He slumped to his knees and pressed his ear against the breast of the sheriff. He could hear nothing. As a matter of fact, his brain was so disturbed that he might not have heard the gallop of a horse.

But this, with the sight of the crimson pool, was enough for Jim Curry. He started to his feet and rushed out of the office, moaning. What unlucky demon had inspired his actions this day of days? In another moment he was on his horse and galloping full speed for his home.

II

Straight out of town and down the road toward the little shack that he called home sped Jim Curry. Plunging from the saddle, he dashed open the door and confronted his son.

The accidental killing of Dad Jackson had sent him rushing to the sheriff to make his confession. The encounter with the sheriff nearly maddened him, for he did not know that the sheriff had not been killed by the fall.

In a single great rush of words he babbled out to his son all that he had done, or thought that he had done.

Jim Curry, the second, listened and said nothing. He was a second edition of his father in many ways. He was equally indolent, equally skillful with his hands and with weapons, equally careless about money and the things money could buy. Indolence, however, so far predominated over other qualities that he had not yet become obnoxious to the world, or perhaps he would outgrow his faults with more years. At present, the whole inner furnishing of his mind came from his father, although quickened and refined by the qualities that had come to him from his mother. He could not, for instance, go blundering and blustering through the village picking fights. He was more apt to sit still all day in the sun, or jog off through the hills on his pony. Physically he was an equal contrast. He was tall, to be sure, but his strength lay in the quality of his wiry muscles rather than in the bulk of them. His hands were excessively long and slender, and they seemed at first glance sheer bone and tendon, without flesh. His face, too, was of a long mold, rather innocuously handsome, as he leaned against the side of the wall and rolled his cigarette. Shaking the tobacco firmly down in it, to give a lip hold, he lighted it and tossed the match through the window. He performed all of these maneuvers without ever taking his eyes from the bowed and swaying form of his father.

"Say something," said the big man at last. "What'll I do? What'll I do?"

The silence that met this appeal caused him to jerk up his head suddenly, as if to curse, but the impassive pair of gray eyes that met his daunted him.

"Well?" he demanded. "What is it, Jimmie? Don't stand there like that, never even winking. It . . . it's too much like your mother, lad. It's like the ghost of her come back to stand there and look at me with the same eyes. She got over being sad. She used to just stand there and watch me and seemed to be waiting. Though what for, except death, I dunno."

He brooded a moment on this, dropping his head so that he did not see the slight shudder pass through the body of his son. When he looked up again, the eyes of Jimmie were grave and emotionless. In truth there was a great gulf between these two, in spite of the relation of father and son.

"You're all your mother," he said. "All your mother and none of me. But ain't you got nothing to say? Any place I can go and cache myself? You'd ought to know the hills like a book. You spent enough time in 'em."

"No use," said the son.

"Eh?"

"It's too late," said the emotionless voice.

"You lie," retorted the father.

"You couldn't hide out in the hills."

"Why not?"

"You'd get lonesome. You ain't the kind to go living off by yourself. You'd miss your friends. Some night you'd ride in to see 'em, and they'd hang you in return."

The father swallowed hard as the truth of this prophecy was borne upon him.

"I'll get out and ride . . . then I'll get distance behind me, anyways."

"That won't do you no good," said the boy. He was hardly nineteen, but his calm exposition of the facts made him seem vastly older. "You ain't got a hoss on the place that'll stand up under a stiff ride for five hours. They'd trail you down before night."

The big man roared in protest: "What's the matter with Bess?"

"You forget about her. You foundered her six weeks ago. I've kept her feet from falling off . . . that's about all."

"Bess gone? I plumb forgot . . . I plumb forgot. But then there's the sorrel, eh?"

"The sorrel? He's gaunted up so's one stiff

ride would about kill him."

"Gaunted up? Why don't you feed the hosses? What else have you got to do?"

"I've told you," said the youth, "that the sorrel can't keep in shape for working unless you'll keep grain to feed him. You ain't had a speck of barley on the place for months."

His father regarded him an accusing glare, as if each fact that had been elicited was another burden to be heaped upon the head of Jimmie, rather than his own.

"Then what d'you think?"

"Only one thing. Stay here and wait for 'em, and, when they come, go with 'em."

The elder man gasped. "Just stand up and let 'em put the rope around my neck, eh? D'you think I'm plumb crazy, boy?"

"It's the best way . . . this going right with 'em," said Jimmie. "You've done wrong enough to run away this far. That's apt to make 'em think all wrong about you."

"Stay here and wait? I suppose you'd do that if you was in my boots?"

"I sure would."

"I kind of believe you would, Jimmie . . . I kind of think you would. You ain't got no red in your veins, just water. But I ain't that kind. I . . . I'd die, Jimmie, if I had to spend a week in a jail. I couldn't breathe inside them cursed walls!"

His son shook his head gravely.

"Ain't you got no feeling?" demanded the father suddenly. "Don't it make no difference to you? You go on smoking like you was at a party." He added bitterly: "Any stranger would do more for me than my own son."

"I'm a poor hand at talking," said Jimmie. "I know that tolerable well."

"Poor at talking and poor in every other way. What've you ever done to help me, or help yourself? What've you ever done, I ask you?"

The cigarette dropped from the fingers of the lad and the paper unfurled and fluttered daintily down to the floor. But Jimmie did not answer. He was thinking intently, and a dark flush gradually mounted to his cheeks.

His father suddenly relented.

"Don't take what I say too serious!" he exclaimed. "You know me, Jimmie. Buck up! I love you, lad, and I'd be with you through thick and thin. D'ye hear?"

His great hand fell on the shoulder of the youth, who looked up, as pale as he had been red the moment before. His eyes were slightly suffused, and his lips trembled. But this show of emotion occurred for only a second and was so slight that his father did not note it. Moreover all things were forgotten a moment later as Jimmie raised his right hand for silence, and into that listening wait poured the drumming of the hoofs of many galloping horses.

Jim Curry rushed to the door, threw it half open, and then staggered back, as if blinded.

"What is it?" asked the son.

"Look for yourself," said the father. "Look for yourself. I've seen enough to suit me. Oh, if that's what they want, they'll find that they're hunting a wolf. They'll sure find that."

By this time Jimmie Curry had slipped to the window and peered out. He found a spectacle fitted to freeze his heart as well as that of his father. Down the road, not a quarter of a mile away, streamed a score and a half of riders, bending over the necks of shimmering horses, wet and foaming with the speed at which they had been ridden the half dozen miles out of the town. The manes blew back against the breasts and shoulders of this group, but, most significant of all, the face of every man was obscured, or partially obscured, by some sort of a mask. With some it was a strip of black cloth, perhaps torn from the linings of their coats. With others it was a bandanna fastened inside the hat, and falling loosely across face, with owlish eye holes cut in it; again the bandanna was drawn up to the eyes, as if they had been riding herd through thick, blowing dust. But, in one shape or another, every man he saw wore a mask, and the meaning was clear. They had come to take the law into their own hands; they had come to strike while the iron was hot.

Jimmie Curry slammed the door shut, locked it, and propped a loose board against it. Then he ran to the small window and drew across it the thin hood of slats, which served to shut out wind and rain, for there was no glass in that primitive habitation.

His father had been busy taking down loaded rifles and revolvers from the well-stocked racks. He turned, gun in hand, to observe his silent, swift-moving son.

"What d'ye mean to do, Jimmie?" he asked.

"Well?" asked the boy in return.

"D'ye mean to stay here and be killed like a rat in a trap? There's no crime on your head, my boy."

"What's crime on your head is crime on mine," answered Jimmie. "I'll stay."

"You fool . . . ," began the father.

He was cut short by the rush of hoof beats around the cabin.

"We've got no time for talk," said Jimmie Curry, and his father stepped to his side and silently wrung his hand.

"Boy," said the elder man, "why ain't we found each other out before this?"

"We been too lazy," answered Jimmie huskily. "But chiefly it was because I ain't much good at talking."

III

Before they could speak again, there was the heavy beat of a hand against the door. "Hello," said a voice outside. "Will you come out, Jim, or do we have to bust down the door and take you?"

The deep hum of agreement that rose from the mob at the end of this speech meant much to the two who listened breathlessly inside. That mob of armed men had been raised suddenly in answer to a fierce impulse when the sheriff was found with a fractured skull, only able to whisper to the first man who found him: "Curry did it and Curry killed Dad Jackson. Get him and . . . ." The sheriff had intended to say: "Do no harm, but put him in jail." But the men did not wait for him to complete his speech. In five minutes, thirty excited fighters were on horseback, pouring out of town. They paused at Jackson's shack, saw the dead body, and continued, hungry to get at the slayer and hang him to the nearest tree.

"What would happen if I opened the door?" asked Jim Curry.

"You'll have to take a chance on that."

A stream of curses was Curry's answer to this suggestion, but he was stopped by the raised hand of his son.

"Who accuses Jim Curry," asked the boy, "of murder?"

"And who's talking so big about Curry? Who's asking?"

"It's the young rat talking for the old rat," answered one of the posse. "It's Jimmie, and by my way of thinking it would be a good thing if we put him out of the way along with his father. He's got the making of the same sort of stuff in him, except that he won't be apt to wait so long before he starts raising trouble."

"You keep your thoughts about Jimmie to yourself," said the first speaker, "until we get our hands on the old man. Then the boy can be taken care of, but nobody's to lay a hand on him until he's done something that calls for trouble."

"Thanks!" called Jimmie Curry. "I sure take that kind of you."

"Keep your thanks. Open the door."

"Show us the warrant for the arrest."

"The warrant for the arrest is the killing he's done. It's warrant enough to suit us."

The growl of assent on the outside fell away as Jimmie called sharply: "The killing that's been done is plumb nothing to the killing that'll take place if you gents try to force that door. We got the guns, and we got the will to shoot. Gents, the minute you lay a hand on that door and try to break it open, you go against the law, and we got a right to shoot in self-defense. There ain't no officer of the law that I hear talking on the outside. If there is, let him come around to the window and show himself."

"And get shot?"

"You know well enough," answered Jimmie hotly, "that, whatever you have against my father and me, you can't say that we ever, eitherof us, have broken our word or took unfair advantage. Isn't that straight?"

"Except murdering white-headed old men."

"Will you hear the truth about that?"

"I'll hear the lies that you got to tell . . . or some of 'em."

"My father was with old Dad Jackson. They was talking about old times. Dad showed a couple of gun tricks. Father done a double roll, and one of the guns went off by mistake. Is that tolerable clear to you?"

"A tolerable clear lie!" shouted someone. "Boys, are you going to let that stand?"

Their cry of denial was ample answer.

"It's going to be a fight, after all," whispered Jimmie softly as he turned to his father. "Here's good bye."

"Lad," murmured the father, "how can I let you stay and . . . ?"

"Hush," said Jimmie. "They're talking it over. Maybe they will change their minds."

For on the outside the men had drawn back and were arguing.

"If we tackle that house," they growled, "there sure is going to be some killing done, and the killing ain't going to fall on our side. They're fighters, both of 'em, and they come out of a fighting stock. Besides, they got the right on their side. They can kill us off like dogs, and it'll still be legal. On the other hand, if we let 'em bluff us out, we'll be laughingstocks. Jeffersonville has had a chance to laugh at our post office, and now it'll sure have a good chance to laugh at the way we go out and capture killers. But it's up to us boys to decide if we want to risk some of our own men?"

The argument ran in this manner, but here it came to a point where a decisive answer had to be made, and the answer was not long in coming. A murmur, a growl, and then it was decided unanimously that so many men would be shamed if they met together, rode to execute vengeance, and then were foiled by the opposition of two wretched men. And one of these was less than a man—he was only a boy.

One more demand that Jim Curry go out to meet them, and then they started to draw back. Jim Curry, watching through a crack, pulled up his Colt to fire, but his son knocked his hand down.

"They ain't going to fire," he assured his father calmly enough.

"Why, you idiot," replied his father, "ain't they

31

getting back into cover behind the woodpile and the barn? What does that mean?"

"They'll just throw a few shots into the top of the shack to try to make you come out," said Jimmie Curry. "They ain't going to open up and fire on this house blindly. Why? Because I'm in here, and one of them shots might hit me."

"D'you think they'd care about that?"

Jimmie flushed with rather scornful anger as he stared at his father. "Of course they care. They ain't murderers, Dad, not a bit of it. They're all heated up, just now. That's all that's wrong with 'em. They think you're a killer and they want to get you. But they ain't going to shoot to kill. They might plug me, and they know that I ain't done nothing."

"It's too late now," replied the elder. "They've all took to shelter. But I tell you, Son, you figure that mob has got brains and thinks. You're all wrong. Them gents out yonder mean to fight until they get me, and, if they have to get you before they get me, why, they'll go right ahead and do it. Nothing can stop 'em. A mob ain't got any more brains than a blind bull."

He had hardly ended before a gun exploded in the near distance, and the report was followed by a rolling volley.

"Shooting through the roof, eh?" shouted Jim Curry excitedly. "Look at that, will you? D'you call that the roof?"

For the bullets had smashed through the walls of the shack, breast high, and in the first glance the two besieged men could distinguish a dozen little round eyeholes, which the slugs had punctured through the thin boards.

Jimmie Curry glanced around, amazed. There was a trickle of crimson down the back of his hand where a bullet had grazed the skin. The wound was of the most trifling nature, but the boy looked down at it as if it had been mortal.

"They are shooting to kill," he said. "They are doing that."

"Didn't I tell you?" asked his father as he threw himself on the floor. "They're shooting to kill, right enough, and, if they don't get us quick enough, they'll fire the shack and plug us by the light of the flames as we run out, because it's getting pretty dark in here now. About sunset time, I think."

Jimmie dropped down beside his father. His Colt was in his hand. "I don't believe it yet!" he exclaimed. "I can't believe it!"

"Can't you? Then look at that . . . curse 'em. They're shooting high and low." As he spoke, bullets began to smash through the sides of the shack only a few inches above the floor. The posse had foreseen, doubtless, that the men inside might lie flat, and they were guarding against that maneuver.

"Get up, Jimmie," said his father. "Get up

before they finish you like a dog. They . . . ."

As he spoke, he was rising to his knees, but he never was able to finish his sentence. His head toppled back and he fell across the body of his son, shot squarely through the temples.

As for Jimmie Curry, he sat for a moment, stunned, with the shoulders of his father in his lap, heedless of the roar of the guns and the noise of the bullets, as they crunched through the sides of the little shack. Then the dead body quivered under the impact of another slug, and Jimmie started to his feet, groaning with rage.

He ran to the window. That side of the house and the door side were commanded by the men hiding behind the woodpile and in the barn. The sun was just below the horizon, but there was still ample light. If there was to be an escape, he must get through on the other side, which would be swept only at an angle by the fire of the besiegers. But that side of the house was blank wall. He rested his hand thoughtfully against the thin boards regardless, or nearly regardless of the hum and smash of bullets around him. They snapped through the very wall before him, and that revealed to him that the thin boards were rotten, that the nails were rusty. Suppose he were to throw himself at those boards at the far end of the shack, close to the place where they were fastened to the beams with the old nails?

In a moment he had put the plan into execution. Starting the full width of the shack, he ran with all his might, threw himself sidewise, his shoulder first, like a football player giving interference, and struck the boards with all his might. They groaned back, far back on the nails. He instantly repeated the attack, regardless of the danger of breaking half of his ribs and injury to his shoulder. The second assault succeeded better than his dreams. In another instant, covered with scratches from the broken ends of the boards, Jimmie rolled head over heels in the sand beyond.

An explosion of a half a dozen guns simultaneously covered the noise of his exit, and, before the posse was aware of his flight, he was on his feet and running at the top of his speed toward a group of horses that the avengers had foolishly left without guard on the road.

The moment they sighted him, sensing at once that he had bolted because the second man was incapacitated by a wound and therefore would not be able to cover the flight, the entire posse rushed from behind the woodpile and out of the barn and poured across the open space after Jimmie.

He had a vital lead, however, and the accuracy of their fire was disturbed by their running, by the poor light, and by the distance. In another moment they dared not fire at all because he was directly in line with the horses. Besides, their only motive in dropping the fugitive was the fear that it might be the elder Curry himself. And when two or three made out for certain that it was the son, they attempted to check the others.

It was hard to check a flood of thirty men, however. They streamed on, shouting and firing their guns, while Jimmie Curry leaped into a saddle, twitched his horse halfway around to avoid a group of its companions, and then, driving his mount into a gallop, whirled and fired pointblank at the pursuers.

One man threw up his arms, fell with a scream, and lay still. Another doubled up in a knot and writhed this way and that, after his tumble.

That spurt of fire drove the pursuers to the ground, and, before they could open and maintain a dangerous fire, young Curry was beyond reach in the rapidly increasing gloom of the evening.

The pursuit that streamed after him was only half-hearted. And ten miles away, shaking off the last of those who hung at his heels, Jimmie Curry looked back and shook his fist from the top of the hill, on which he sat his stolen horse, to the glimmering lights of the village in the hollow below.

His hand, indeed, was against all the rest of the world. They had murdered his father, and he in turn, as he then thought, had killed two of the slayers. Afterward he was to learn that neither of them had died of their wounds. But when he learned this, it was too late to take him from the course to which he committed himself.

Without rudder or purpose, he was sent adrift. He could not even properly avenge the fall of his father. Masked men had killed him—that he knew—and two of those masked men had fallen in exchange.

So it was that Jim Curry the second set his face to the world for the first time.

IV

Six years had come and gone over the head of the village of Chester in the Southland. A thousand miles north, on a fresh day in May, the stagecoach rolled with beat of hoofs and rumble of wheels down a steep grade, roared across the inevitable bridge at the bottom of the gulch, and then labored up the other slope. It was a stiff climb. The bright, hot sun of the mountains and the hard lug upgrade started the horses steaming and grunting before they had gone a hundred yards; they were so badly spent when they reached a nearly level stretch of road, winding up the mountain, that the stage driver halted the coach to give his nags a chance to catch their wind.

"It's the green feed," he said commiseratingly to his passengers, swinging around in the seat and dangling one heavily booted leg over the side. This maneuver displayed spurs. Why a stage driver should wear spurs no one of his passengers could guess, and the driver knew as little as they. "It's the green feed," he said, "that knocks the stuffing out of a hoss. Makes 'em all soft and mushy. They got no heart when they come off pasture. Takes a couple of weeks of work and graining 'em before they're up to mountain work. Look at old Bess, that near leader. She's the best of the lot when she gets ripe. But it'll take her another month to round into shape. A plumb crime, I say, to catch a hoss up and send him into the traces right out of the pasture. Ain't I right, chief?"

The chief thus appealed to was a leathery, tobacco-chewing individual, very tall, very slender, and gaily dressed. He was busy manufacturing a cigarette, for he was engaged every moment of the day in smoking a cigar, a cigarette, or chewing tobacco. He alternated these forms of the same diversion. His little, bright-blue eyes glittered down the slope, then turned and dwelt on his companion, the stage driver.

"I dunno," he said. "All I know is that I want to get through to Baxter City, and I want to get through before dark. The Red Devil is around these parts. Be soft for him to land us if he got a chance in the dark."

There were two schoolteachers-to-be in the stage, brown-faced, mountain girls with eyes as big and gentle and timorous as the eyes of deer. They caught their breath at this ominous speech. The third occupant of the stagecoach was an old rancher, whose single ornament was a wallet so stuffed with money that it swelled against the side of his coat. Age had taken the hair from his head, leaving a red, polished skin, with a sparse tuft of white whiskers decorating the end of his chin. His mouth was continually pressed tight, partly because of the uncompromising sternness of his character, partly because he was toothless. The fourth passenger was a youth in his middle twenties, a handsome fellow in a coat that fitted so well around the collar and shoulders that it could have been picked at a great distance as a tailor-made garment. He was a gay, careless chap, one of the sort that girls are apt to look kindly upon. The two incipient schoolteachers had more than once glanced closely at him, but each time they had chosen an occasion when he seemed to be occupied with other things, but he was perfectly aware of every glance that came in his direction. Charlie Mark had been raised in a rough school, the West of the cattle country, but he had chosen a different environment for the display of his talents.

He had wandered East, drifted halfway through several preparatory schools, which fitted him for nothing in particular, and finally, having gone into one business after another, he had abandoned the paths of toil and entered those of ease. In a word, he had become a gambler, a cardsharp of the first water, as he thought. And, indeed, with a little more practice, a little more dexterity gained through patience, he might have made himself into an eminent cheat. Industry, however, was by no means a part of young Mark's natural endowment, and he saw no need of cultivating it. His father, in the West, would come to his aid when he was pinched. But that father had been worn out by the long succession of appeals for aid, and finally he balked at the most embarrassing moment possible for Charlie. There had been a game of infinite possibilities. Charlie was among youngsters who were blessed with more money than they knew how to spend and a seeming desire that Charles Mark should show them how to get rid of it.

Nothing stood in his way but time. They were willing to play high, but they did not wish to play long, and Charlie, working with desperate energy to reap the golden harvest, made one ruinous step, misread a card that he himself had distinctly daubed, and, while holding a full house himself, had called what he believed to be a bluff flush in the hand of a young millionaire. Unfortunately the flush proved to be as good as gold and Charles was thoroughly trimmed.

This undeserved blow smashed his financial position to small bits. He sent a volley of telegrams to the old man and received in return a curt message that the bottom of the gold mine had been reached. Before he got more money, Charles would have to come home and work for it. Driven by the desperate predicament in which he found himself, Charlie obeyed, and he was even now in the last stage of the journey. But so grim was the reception that he knew would await him when he confessed that he needed the money to pay a gambling debt, that, slow though the horses trudged, they went as fast as a bird to the mind of Charlie Mark. Yet he must go on. Those debts must be met. They were contracted in a circle where, if he were once exposed, he could never raise his head again among those who played for high stakes in the games of gentlemen.

A dozen times he had turned this horrible predicament back and forward in his mind. $20,000 would save him, and $20,000 to Charlie Mark seemed a small thing. But, if he asked his father for that sum, there would be a howl that would split the heavens. And how could he explain to the old-fashioned man that he was on the verge of a gold mine that was better than a gold mine in the hills? The $20,000 was simply the can opener with which he could help himself to a big fortune. Certainly after this experience he would never again make a mistake with his daubs.

So bitter was the struggle that was going on inside his mind that he barely heard the words of the tall man who had climbed onto the driver's seat. He asked negligently: "Who's The Red Devil?"

The stage driver looked at the tall man, and the tall man looked at the stage driver. Obviously they were incredulous. It did not seem possible that they could have the good luck to find one who had not heard the stories of The Red Devil.

"The Red Devil," said the driver at length, "is the real article of outlaw, gunfighter, murderer, and . . . ."

"Oh," exclaimed one of the teachers, "are you sure about him being a murderer?"

"Am I sure my name's Jake Trowbridge?" asked the driver, angered by the interruption. "Who killed the Twombly boys, all three of 'em? Who killed Jud Perkins? Who waited all night in the house of Judge Ross and shot his head off when he came home? Who done them things and a hundred more like 'em?"

"I don't know," said the girl who had first spoken. "I don't think that anyone knows. Those dead men were found, and no one knew who the murderer was. They laid the crime to The Red Devil. For my part, I think . . . ."

"Trouble with you young folks is that you think too much!" exclaimed the angered Mr. Trow-

42

bridge. "Or else you think you think. You know more'n growed-up men, you do . . . about things that womenfolks ain't supposed to know nothing about. Who else killed 'em, and a pile more besides them, if The Red Devil didn't?"

"I know," said the girl's companion, flushing with the warmth of her emotion, "that when Christmas came down at . . . ."

"Oh, say," exclaimed the driver, "I'm sure plumb tired of them stories about The Red Devil and what he does for the poor! A gent would think that he took to robbing like a sort of saint. That it? He's too good to live like other folks and work for his money. He takes the coin away from other gents and gives it to them that need it. That what you was going to say?"

"Exactly," said the girl, flushing because she knew that her position was absurd, but, with feminine obstinacy, ready to grit her teeth and stick to the first thing she had maintained. "Isn't it true that the only people he ever robs are miners who have dug their money out of claims they jumped, or ranchers who got their start by rustling cows, or sharpers who win at cards through crooked tricks?"

At the last item in the catalog it seemed to Charlie Mark, who was a trifle sensitive on the subject, that the tall man on the driver's seat started a little and made an involuntary motion toward the inner pocket of his coat. He recovered

43

himself at once, however, and swiftly scanned the faces below him to see if his confusion had been noted. But Charlie Mark was sufficiently adept in the game of chance to make his face a blank and stare blandly up at the driver.

"Maybe that's partly, true," Jake was confessing. "Leastwise I've heard considerable about it. But I put it down for a yarn that ain't got no bottom to it. Lemme see a hold-up gent, a safe blower, a stage robber like The Red Devil that'll turn down any kind of money once he has a chance to put his hands on it."

"Just because he has never been in this exact part of the country," said the girl, "you can say that, and no one will be able to dispute you, but. . . ."

"*Bah!*" replied Jake, putting an end to a conversation in which he was not maintaining the upper hand. The long lash of his whip curled over the backs of his team while he released the brake with a slam.

The well-trained team leaned with a single impulse into the collar, took the back roll of the heavy wagon, and then sent it lurching up the grade, with a smooth and even effort.

During the conversation the old rancher had seemed to sleep. But now he opened his eyes slightly and regarded the two girls, who were murmuring indignantly together, with a tolerant and kindly smile.

"Them are the kind," he remarked suddenly, "that make the world go 'round."

Charlie Mark gazed in lazy tolerance at the girls, who flushed furiously under this encomium.

"Maybe," said Charlie, "you're right." And he yawned.

V

The yawn caused the old rancher to bring his toothless jaws together with such force and suddenness that, had the teeth been present, they would have clicked together with ominous loudness. Little points of light gleamed in his eyes, and for a long moment he stared steadily into the face of Charlie Mark without saying a word. Then, very much in the manner of one who feels that further words are useless, he closed his wrinkled old eyelids and slept or seemed to sleep. Still, perhaps, thoughts were running dreamily through his brain, and it was a comfortable thing for Charlie Mark that he could not read the mind of his traveling companion.

"Anyways," the tall man on the driver's seat was saying to Jake, "he can't really be up here. It was only a couple of days ago that he was down to Chalmerston, and that must be nigh onto two hundred miles away from here."

"That was exactly four days ago come tonight," said the stage driver firmly. "I'd ought to know because I got a brother down there, and he wrote to me all about what The Red Devil done."

"Well," persisted the tall man, "who could make two hundred miles in four days through these mountains, on roads like this? Can you tell me that?"

"Sure I can tell you that. The Red Devil is his name."

"Eh?"

"You asked me a question, and I told you. The Red Devil on his white hoss, Meg, can sure travel as fast as that."

"He can, eh?"

"Sure he can. That Meg hoss is as fast as the wind, and they ain't no wear out to her."

"Then," said the tall man in a sudden fury of exasperation, "why don't you get your team along the road? Want 'em to rest between steps?"

The driver regarded his companion with dull eyes, and then looked carefully over the tall wheel before he answered. "These hosses will go just as fast as is good for 'em and not faster."

"Your company ain't got a right to advertise certain times, and then not make 'em. You'd get fired *pronto*, Jake, if they knew the way you just lazied along the road."

"Maybe I would," said the other, "but you ain't the company, and you can't fire me. You

46

lay onto that, and don't forget it. In the meantime, these hosses ain't going to be killed to get you safe into town, you and your . . . ."

The suddenly raised forefinger of the tall man cut this last part of the sentence into a mutter that cannot be divided into intelligible words. But the unspoken words seemed to contain a threat that effectually reduced the tall man to silence, and, although he frequently stirred uneasily in his place and many times glanced up into the darkening sky of the evening, he did not again venture on an audible protest.

They should have reached the end of this stage of the journey by sundown, but, as a matter of fact, it was between sunset and dusk before they sighted the little village in the distance. At this time they were swaying through a tall-sided gulch, where the road turned over the shoulder of the mountain. It was a short cut, seldom used even by such a skillful driver as Jake, for the trees jutted far out from the banks of the little gorge, and falling limbs, from time to time, were apt to block the way when the wild storms came over the mountain top.

"Now," said Jake over his shoulder, glancing back to his passengers, as he whirled the whip, "we're going to go down this here mountainside a pile faster that we've traveled any other part of this trip."

He followed this with a whoop, and the stage

47

lurched forward at a dizzy pace, while the brakes suddenly jumped into place and made sure, with much screeching of leather pads against the iron tires, that the burden of the stage would not roll down and overmaster the horses. In this manner they swung over the crest of the shoulder of the mountain and were shooting at high and increasing speed under an overhanging scrub oak, when a man's body dropped out of the branches and, with the agility and surety of a panther, landed in the driver's seat.

He had so calculated his fall that his knees struck the shoulders of the tall man and sent him catapulting into the body of the stage, while the newcomer himself retained his balance most precariously and was barely in time to shove a revolver against the throat of Jake, as the latter veteran made a valiant effort to reach his gun. A second revolver was directed into the coach, where the tall man of the gay attire lay gasping and groaning from his fall, and the two girls were moaning their terror. Only the old rancher and Charlie Mark were fairly unperturbed. The former sat quietly erect, with his patient eyes directed calmly into the distance, paying no heed to the armed intruder who had so suddenly plunged down on them and taken control. As for Charlie Mark, there was no fear in his nature.

"He just nacherally lives on excitement," his father had always said, "and he's got to have his share of it, or shrivel up and die like a flower without water. That's the kind Charlie is."

He sat erect now, his eyes bright with happiness, and finally he looked down at the writhing tall man and laughed aloud. "Get up, you fool," he said. "You aren't killed."

The stage in the meantime had been brought to a halt at the command of the newcomer, and Charlie Mark for the first time had a chance to scrutinize him carefully. There was no doubt about his identity. His face was covered entirely by a black mask, but neither mask nor hat entirely covered the flaming red hair that thrust out here and there. This, of course, was The Red Devil, about whom their conversation of that afternoon had so opportunely turned.

As far as could be made out by his voice and by his carriage and build, he was a young man, not much older than Charlie Mark himself. He had sprung down from the driver's seat to the ground, as soon as the vehicle was halted, and from this position he addressed the members of the company and ordered all weapons to be thrown down to him at once. The command was obeyed by the driver, who promptly threw down two huge, old-style Colts, and by the tall man, who cast down the revolver that was hanging at his right thigh.

But The Red Devil was not satisfied. "Look here, Lang," he said, "you can't fool me. I want that other gat. Do I get it?"

"What other gat?" asked the tall man, who The Red Devil knew as Lang. "I ain't got another gun."

The robber shrugged his shoulders. He stood so negligently graceful, resting his weight more on the right leg than on the left, that, had it not been for the long pair of guns in his hands, he would have seemed a casual gossip, exchanging news by the way. The guns, however, gave him significance.

"I ain't got time to talk," he said. "Shell out, Lang."

"How can I shell out when I ain't got a gun?" demanded the tall man.

"You dog!" exclaimed the other with sudden heat. "Why I waste so much time on you . . . why I don't turn you into buzzard meat right off, I dunno. Throw that gun out, or I'll turn you into a sieve!"

"All right," said Lang. "I see you got pretty sharp eyes, partner. Here you are."

As he spoke, he produced another weapon from his clothes and made as if to toss it to the ground. The gesture, however, terminated in bringing the little automatic whirling around in his fingertips, and fire spurted from the muzzle. It was a neat shot, swiftly executed, and Charlie Mark saw the sombrero jerk up and then down on the head of the bandit. From the latter's bigger gun, drowning with its report the screaming of the two girls, came a bullet that caused the gun to drop from the right hand of the tall man, and he bowed over, cursing with pain. The little automatic *clattered* to the ground.

"You're, lucky, and I'm lucky," said The Red Devil. "You're lucky that I ain't going to kill you for a treacherous hound, Lang, and I'm lucky that snap shot didn't tear the top of my hat off. I guess I won't need to put any air holes in this here sombrero, eh?"

He changed his cold tone. "Ladies," he said, "will you fix up Lang's arm? He ain't going to die. He's just got a clip through the upper arm, about a couple of inches above the elbow. Be as well as ever he was in a couple of weeks. Can you turn a bandage around it for me? Thanks. You got nothing to be afraid of."

They obediently stripped the coat from Lang, while The Red Devil turned some of his attention to the old rancher.

"Well, pop," he said, "here you are again. Seems like you and me are bound to keep meeting up, eh? You still got that old gat of yours?"

"Sure I got it, son," said the rancher. "I got it stowed away where it'll stay put, less'n you start bothering me, boy."

"I ain't going to bother you, pop," said the outlaw. "Not a bit. You got about eight thousand on your hip, I happen to know, along with that gun, but you'd give me eight-thousand-dollars' worth of trouble before I got through with you, if I took it."

At the mention of this large sum the eyes of the rancher suddenly widened and as suddenly contracted. But at length, breathing hard, he nodded.

"I guess you know the facts, son," he said. "All I got to say is that it ain't fear that keeps you from taking it, but because you know it's honest money, lad. Well, the time may come . . . ."

"Sure it may," said the outlaw, interrupting good naturedly. "And when it does come, I'll drop around and let you know what you can do to help me. Will you throw me that coat of Lang's, ladies?"

They obeyed, tossing the coat so that it fell at the feet of the outlaw. He kicked it into the air with the toe of his boot and caught it in his left hand.

Lang in the meantime raised a shrill complaint. "There'll be two families starving this winter if you take what's in there," he declared. "That represents the money I got by slaving and. . . ."

"You yaller hound," said the outlaw through his set teeth. "I got a mind to tell these folks how you come by that money, and, if you yap again, I will."

The threat caused the mouth of the miserable

Lang to close, as if the jaws were glued. Trembling with sorrow and anxious care, like a wet dog in a cold wind, he watched the outlaw toss the coat over his arm.

"I got some attention to pay to the lining," explained The Red Devil. "You'll have to ride cold the next stage of your trip, Lang. I want the other ten thousand."

So saying, he stepped back and whistled. The answer was most surprising. Down the precipitous slope of the gulch, like a mountain sheep, came a white horse, a dazzling vision in the dimness. It paused at the side of The Red Devil, and the latter, vaulting into the saddle, turned to flee.

VI

"Shoot!" cried Lang, turning eagerly to the rancher. "If you got a gun, let's see you use it. Shoot and shoot to kill. That's The Red Devil! Twenty thousand to you, if you get him . . . dead or alive. That's the reward they've offered."

The old rancher drew out his revolver, but it seemed to watchful Charlie Mark that he moved with unnecessary deliberation, and, when he fired, Charlie could tell that it was a random shot that did not cause the fugitive even to look around over his shoulder. Lang, groaning with rage, tore the weapon from it's owner with his left hand and opened fire, but by this time the swiftly moving white horse had carried the outlaw into the veil of darkness, and he was safe.

"You might have drilled him clean," said Lang, casting down the revolver with an oath and flinging himself back into a seat. "You might have finished him easy, if you'd wanted to. Why didn't you want to? Because you're running in the same gang with him. That's how you get your money. By heaven, I'd swear to it. You and him are in cahoots. How else does he learn what he knows about the folks that travel in this here stagecoach?"

The rancher listened calmly to this tirade. "Did I ever see you before you climbed into this stage?" he asked.

As the answer to this question would have torn the theory of Lang to shreds, he made no answer, but with a groan proffered his arm to the girls to complete the bandage.

They finished a hasty job, during which he turned his attention and his complaints to the driver, who was now down picking up his guns and shoving them back into the holsters with the greatest equanimity.

"And I suppose," said Lang, "that all I'll get out of the stage company will be that they're sorry. Is that it? You run your stage through a gang of outlaws and don't send no guard, and. . . ."

"You've talked enough," said Jake with sudden anger. "If you got any more talking to do, let's hear why you sew up your money in the lining of your coat. And let's hear how you got that money? Seemed like you weren't none too anxious to have The Red Devil tell about it a while back."

Lang looked about him with wicked eyes and twitching lips, but, from the cold face of the rancher to the angered face of Jake and the openly contemptuous face of Charlie Mark, he found no ally. Eventually, giving no thanks to the teachers for their care, he dropped back in his place and dropped his forehead into the palm of his left hand.

And only then did the old rancher look to Charlie Mark, raise his eyebrows, and smile ever so faintly. Plainly he felt they were more or less akin, and that this tall fellow was a stranger in their midst. The insinuation in some way shrewdly flattered young Mark.

He fell into a brown study in the meantime. Vaguely, on either side and before him, he heard the shrill, pleasant voices of the girls and the growls of Jake and the groans of Lang. They were busily commenting on the hold-up in all of its phases, from the hair-raising daring of that drop out of the overhanging scrub oak to the appearance of the beautiful white horse. But, although Charlie Mark was thinking of the same subject, he was concentrating on it with such prodigious intentness that he actually heard not a word of the conversation of the others.

There were many strange features about the affair. In the first place, there he sat, a sure shot, a truly deadly hand with a revolver with a weapon in his clothes, and yet from the first glimpse of that red hair above the mask, he had not even dreamed of resistance. If he had had money in any large sum with him, it might have been otherwise, and he assured himself that it would have been otherwise. But in his heart of hearts he knew that he would not have had the hardihood to oppose The Red Devil for an instant. The man was too formidable to be encountered.

His own easy surrender was one thing, and that of Jake was another. Jake Trowbridge was not a light-handed fellow by any means, and yet Jake had apparently no more dreamed of fighting back than had Charlie Mark. The old rancher was another. He, it seemed, had been an eyewitness of the doings of the bandit before this date. And what he had seen had convinced him that resistance was foolish. Yet he was a grim old chap, and certainly he was the sort to fight for money, even for a nickel, to say nothing of $8,000.

But what of Lang? He fought back, but only in desperation. In fact, the marvel of the affair was that so many fearless fighting men could have been so completely dominated by another that, from the first, resistance seemed madness.

And how was it done?

Doubtless the outlaw was a marksman of the most accurate nicety, as witness the consummate skill with which he had sent his shot through the gun arm of Lang, and then had calmly called his shot to the fraction of an inch. It was astounding that he could afford to shoot to disarm in such a crisis, instead of merely shooting to kill. Yet Charlie Mark was no mean marksman himself, and in time, if he had to use a revolver for the sake of his safety and his livelihood, he might attain to a similar degree of power with weapons.

It was not the weapon, however, that had made The Red Devil so tremendously commanding a figure from his first appearance in the coach. It was simply his reputation. He was The Red Devil, and that name was to him both sword and shield. Men were disarmed by the mention of it. His battle was won by his appearance. Perhaps he had done mighty things in the first place to build up this repute, but certain it was that he need do nothing now.

These thoughts were turning around and around in the active brain of Charlie Mark as he entered the village in the coach. He dismounted from it so absent-mindedly that he hardly heard the exclamations that poured out around him on all sides.

But first he announced that he was not going to use the rest of his ticket, and he sold it to the first man who wished to go on from that point. Next he went to the hotel and secured a room for the night. Having done this, he went directly to the blacksmith shop and secured from the black-smith, in whose corral he had seen some fine horses, a lithe-limbed young chestnut that seemed to have both endurance and speed. Saddle and bridle were added from the diminishing store of Charlie's money.

He went back to the hotel and flung himself on his bed for a sleep as deep as if he were stunned. In the morning he got up, breakfasted, saddled, and rode away before the gray of dawn had turned into a rosier light.

The plan, which had formed in his mind during the trip into the village after the hold-up, had grown there during the evening, and at length he was determined to make the desperate effort.

His needs were $20,000 at once. Such a sum he could hardly expect to receive from his father. Without that amount of money he could never go East and step back into the place he had recently abandoned. From the short dialogue between The Red Devil and Lang, he gathered that a sum as large as this, or nearly as large, must be the spoil of the robber for this single, easy feat.

Gambling was a profitable pursuit, but it seemed to be nothing compared with this profession of outlawry. And the determination of Charlie Mark, to put it shortly, was to take the trail of the robber, run him down, and hold him up, just as he, The Red Devil, held up the rest of the world.

It was a sufficiently rash determination, but Charlie Mark had been reduced to a position fully as desperate. He must have that money, and, as he drew nearer to his home and his father, he realized more and more fully that the grim old man would never supply him with half this amount. Moreover, the bare demand would ruin his credit at home forever. The little bald-headed rancher, sitting opposite him in the coach, had reminded him forcibly of his father. What the one would not give, the other would not give. And who could imagine the man with the red, polished skin, the hairless face, giving $20,000 to pay off a gambling debt?

Reflections such as these had determined Mark to take the step, but he was so good a man of action that, once he had made up his mind, he dismissed his anxiety. Riding out of the village in the cold, morning light, he had a song bubbling on his lips. Of course there was barely one chance in a hundred that he could even find a clear trail. But he gambled on that chance, and, going straight to the gulch, he found it easy to pick up the beginning of the stranger's flight.

VII

The continuation, however, was by no means so simple as the opening of the trail. All day he rode through the mountains, sometimes stumbling off of what he thought to be the trail, and sometimes coming back on it. The dimness of the evening found him saddle weary and saddle sore in a district that was perfectly unfamiliar to him.

He began to find that his long absence from the West and the ways of the West had turned him into a veritable tenderfoot. Not only was his eye dulled, but his strength had been sapped by dissipation in the East. And now, with the first shadows of night swinging across the valley in which he found himself, he gave up his task, turned about, and struck at random on what he thought was the back trail toward the village from which he had started. Presently the chill certainty struck him that he must spend the night in the wilderness.

In this gloomy mood, careless of the way his horse took after that long day of anxious hope and searching, he began to climb the steep side of the hill and was halfway to the top when the scent of frying bacon hurried him to the crest and opened his eyes in the hope of finding the nearby house from which the tempting odor had proceeded. To his utter astonishment, however, there was no habitation in sight. He rubbed his eyes and peered again on all sides, but still he could see no sign of a habitation. To be sure the shadows of the evening had deepened to such a degree that he could not distinguish objects at any considerable distance, but certainly he could look far enough to have detected the origin of that pleasant scent of bacon.

But, so far as he could tell, the odor came literally out of the ground. He stared in bewilderment at the hillside. There was no orifice. There was nothing among that litter of vast boulders to indicate the entrance to a cave, or a lean-to put up against one of the rocks. His horse, too, began to lift and cock its head, as it smelled the food of man, which, in the natural course of events, ought to include its own share of fodder. And such was Charlie Mark's amazement at his situation that he allowed the animal to retrace its steps down the side of the hill.

Halfway to the bottom the horse paused, and Charlie Mark, thinking that the animal might have come by instinct to the root of the mystery, examined the situation carefully. But there was no hint of a dwelling of men, or even of an open-air campfire. Indeed the scent of frying bacon was gone entirely. Mark turned the horse, therefore, and, with an oath of exasperation drove it at a cruel gallop up the steep crest. But here he brought it to a halt once more, with a wrench at the reins that made the poor beast throw up its head and half rear with the suddenness of its stop. The odor had returned out of the barren rocks.

Charlie Mark threw himself off the horse and knelt. But the scent immediately disappeared. Half frantic with this will-o'-the-wisp odor, he flung himself into the saddle again and sat, musing, when, to his surprise, the horse for a second time turned and wandered slowly down among the boulders of the side of that rude gulch. This time when the animal halted, Charlie Mark dismounted, determined to investigate more thoroughly. He advanced not according to what he saw, but according to the direction in which the head of the horse pointed. Presently he came to an immense boulder, fully twenty feet high and fitting solidly into the side of the gorge. Rather than a rock, it seemed an outcropping, as if here the broken ends of strata projected through the thin outer masking of soil.

With a scowl Charlie Mark considered this unprepossessing monster, and then moved around to the side of the rock. There was a narrow crevice, not more than two feet wide, he thought, or three at the most, between the right side of the huge rock and the hill. He stepped to it and found that there was nothing but sheer blackness within. He reached out, expecting that his hand would strike the rough surface of the stone, but his arm fell through an arc of thin air. With a stifled grunt of surprise, Charlie Mark advanced a long pace, holding out his hand, but still there was no sign of reaching an end of the passage.

Here he stopped, drew his revolver, and made sure that it was ready for firing. Raising his hands above his head, he had made out that the rock was squared away in a manner most unusual for the careless natural chisels of wind and weather. In fact, he could almost swear that he had felt the places that had been nicked out with hammer and drill.

Armed and prepared for whatever might come, he found that the passage suddenly terminated in the original direction, but veered to the right. He followed for five or six steps, turned again, and in another moment he was at the entrance of a commodious cave, some seven feet in height and fifteen feet or more in breadth, that extended an unknown distance into the bosom of the hill.

It was rudely fitted out as a dwelling and stable. In the distance he saw the glimmering figure of the white horse, and to the right and left saddles and guns leaned against the wall or were suspended from it. Altogether there was equipment for quite an establishment, and the whole was set off and fitfully illuminated by the blaze of a small fire, which glowed and darted up small flames from between two rocks. The pans scattered about showed that it was the cooking fire, and the only human being in sight was at once the cook and the diner.

He was a young fellow of not more than twenty-five years, brown faced, wide-shouldered, handsome in a lean-featured way, with a restless habit of hands and eyes. Charlie Mark regarded him with great interest. Why he did not at once advance and announce himself, he could not afterward be sure, but there was something about the silence with which the other sat there that detained him, and in another instant Charlie Mark saw a thing that was sure to keep him quiet. It was no more or less than a shimmering wig of red hair—flame-red hair—hanging from the pommel of a saddle on the wall.

Beyond any doubt it identified the solitary cave dweller. Indeed, it seemed to Charlie Mark, now that he knew, that he should have been able to distinguish the robber, even without the wig, by his build and a certain energy of movement, snake-like for suddenness, cat-like for grace.

This was The Red Devil in his permanent abode, and luck had brought Charlie Mark to it —luck and the instinct of his wise-headed horse. Somewhere in this cave must be hidden no end of treasure. For many years now, as he gathered from the conversation he had heard in the stage-coach, The Red Devil had been the terror of the mountains and he must have stored up immense amounts of loot. And what more secure cache than this cave, where he had been willing to trust his own person, as the furnishings of the place showed? Without more ado, Charlie Mark raised his revolver and took careful aim.

But as he held it, the outlaw stiffened and turned his head, with a suddenness that caught the breath of young Mark. He saw that lean, handsome face, intent with listening, and he saw large, glowing-bright eyes fixed upon him. So it seemed at least, although the intervening walls of shadow must, of course, make him invisible to the outlaw. Yet Charlie Mark lowered the gun and waited, only praying that he would not be discovered.

He was not, and presently The Red Devil turned again to his plate of food.

Mark decided that he must get nearer for his shot, and consequently nearer he crept, nearer and nearer until the light of the little fire began to play faintly on his hands. He was moving with the most painstaking care, his revolver thrusting forward with every move of the right hand; there was no possible sound, yet half a dozen times as he drifted along, he saw the other straighten and stiffen in alarm and listen. But he did not again turn, apparently using reason to club his alert senses back into a false sense of security.

What an equipment of hair-trigger nerves the

fellow must have. And in the meantime, thought Mark, what if he shot the man, and then were unable discover the site on which he had buried the treasure? The last thought was enough to stop the beating of his heart. Should he attempt to hold up this expert fighter? Should he attempt to cover him with the gun and then, having tied him, draw out the information he wanted, promising in return freedom?

It would be easy to promise freedom. He could forget his promise, once he had located the loot. But that money he must have. It was not enough, now, that the reward on the head of The Red Devil, alive or dead, would just clear his gambling debts. The buried money must be brought out into the light of day where it would serve Charlie Mark, as he had always yearned to be served, with a sufficient capital to start gambling on a large scale. With the proper backing to start with, he had the dexterity of wits and fingers to enable him to pry open the richest wallets in the land.

Now he was not twenty feet away, and, rising to his knees and thence to a crouching position, he presented his revolver and covered the outlaw securely.

"Hands up!"

The first word made the head of the outlaw jerk up. Then, although Mark saw the swelling of the tensed muscles along the shoulders, the robber

66

did not stir save to raise his hands slowly. At the shoulders they hesitated and seemed to be fighting, and then again they rose to the position of helplessness above his head. With wonderful nerve, he managed to sit looking steadily away from the danger behind him.

Charlie Mark admired him from the bottom of his cold heart. What a gambler this man would have made!

He picked up from the ground the noose end of a fallen lariat, and, with left-handed dexterity, he threw it. Fair and true it dropped over the shoulders of the outlaw and squeezed against his side the arms, the raised elbows that were still below the level of the shoulders.

There was a stifled curse from the outlaw, and that was all. At the exultant command of Charlie Mark, he rose and stood patiently while Mark relieved him of gun and knife. Then obediently he turned and took his place on the stone near the wall, which Charlie pointed out.

VIII

Mark now kicked a quantity of wood onto the fire. As the flames rose, illuminating the cave, he sat down in comfort and looked at his victim. It was a vastly more thrilling thing to confront those big, brilliant eyes, he found, than to look into the face of the richest gambler in the world. The stakes were money on one hand, life on the other. And life, for some reason, seemed more precious than coin, an observation that the hard-headed Charlie had never before made.

He was taking no chances. His long revolver was balanced across the top of his knees and directed at the breast of the other. He kept his grip on it secure. His back against the solid wall gave him security from attack in that direction. There was nothing to fear except from the helpless man who sat confronting him, a few feet away. The game was won, and yet, with the surety at hand, Charlie Mark was still not altogether confident.

"The queer thing," he said at length, "is that no one else has been able to do this."

"I can tell you how that happened," said the other without the slightest tremor of fear escaping to temper his voice. "I simply left the block of stone out of the entrance tonight. If it hadn't been for that, I guess you wouldn't be here now, eh, partner?"

"I guess not," admitted Charlie Mark.

"You wouldn't be here. You'd be clear on the other side, away from twenty thousand dollars' worth of man?" He grinned as he spoke. Then he continued: "Well, what's the main idea, friend? You take me into town tonight, or do you sleep out here?"

"Sleep out here!" exclaimed Charlie Mark. "You sure figure me to be green, sir."

"Tolerable green," The Red Devil said insolently.

"But not green enough to try to sleep here in the cave with you . . . not while you're alive."

He threw in the sinister hint with a marked change in his voice. But The Red Devil merely smiled.

"Would you have me dead in here?" he said. "Would you have the nerve to sleep with a dead man?"

"Why not," asked Charlie Mark, "when you're worth as much dead as you are alive they say."

"Do they say that? Well, they lie."

"Let the money go. I have enough of that, and. . . ."

"You're out for the glory of taking me, eh?"

"That's it!"

"You lie," said the outlaw, sneering. "You're here for the money . . . you want hard cash. You're on a trail like a ferret, and you won't get off till you have your teeth deep in. I know you."

He spoke with the most remarkable assurance, and Charlie Mark felt as guilty as if some confidant had informed the man of what went on in his secret mind, and yet to no confidant had he murmured a syllable of his plans. It was uncanny.

"What made you think that?"

"Well, a bird whispered it to me."

"Listen," replied Charlie Mark, "you're money in my pocket, either as dead meat or live stuff. I don't much care which. Now talk when I tell you to. What made you think I'd come here just for the money. Out with it."

The other regarded him with an unfaltering sneer. And it was plain that he answered not because he was in fear, but because he chose to speak.

"You're tolerable scared," he said, "but even in spite of being scared, you keep looking around. I know that you half expect to see a pile of gold sacks."

Charlie Mark gritted his teeth. "Well, my friend," he said, "I'm glad you have such a handy sense of humor."

"I can laugh," answered the brigand. "That's something that I learned early."

"Well," said Charlie Mark, trembling with anger at this continued sneering, "you'd better crowd a lot of laughing into the next few minutes. Your time's short."

"No," answered the other. "You're hound enough, I guess, to shoot a gent deliberately, but, before you pull the trigger, you'll take another think and begin to worry about the loot you may be missing if you kill me now."

"Can't I dig up the whole length of the cave and find it?" asked Charlie Mark.

"Sure you can dig up the whole floor of the cave, but what makes you so sure that the coin is buried here? Do you think that a wise gent would live in the same place in which he kept his coin? That'd be a fool idea, I figure!"

"Hmm," replied Charlie Mark. "You think on all sides of things, I see."

"For you and against you," said The Red Devil.

"Right now," Charlie Mark stated, resting his elbows on his knees, "you're pretty sure you're going to get out of this mess alive and happy. Why?"

"Because," said The Red Devil, whose hair, by the way, was a very ordinary dark brown, "because I can't see myself being killed by a rat like *you*."

"Curse you!" cried Charlie Mark, springing to his feet. "I think you're hungry to die!"

"Bah," said the other sneeringly. "Don't point that gun at me. You won't shoot. You're a gold-digger, that's what you are."

Charlie Mark stepped back writhing with rage and the knowledge that the outlaw had read him right. It was true. He dared not take the chance and kill when there might be thousands and thousands of dollars within the reach of this fellow's cleverness. With his hate there was mingled a great and growing admiration.

"Anyway," said Charlie Mark, "the stuff you took from Lang must be here, and that, together with the coin on your head, is enough for me."

"If you're as cheap as that . . . go ahead. I rated you a little higher. A little too high, I guess."

A stream of curses burst from the lips of Charlie Mark, curses because he wished with all his head to drive a volley of lead slugs into the body of his tormentor, and yet he had not the nerve to do it.

"I'll hear you talk a while," he said. "What d'you got to say?"

"Nothing much."

"Hurry it up," said Charley Mark. "I haven't a year's time on my hands."

The Red Devil laughed.

Charlie Mark listened in awe and pleasure. There was never in the world a sound so silken, he felt. It flowed and rippled from the throat of the robber. It was a thing of wonder and of beauty, and it was hardly louder than a whisper. It brought the white horse leisurely from the rear of the cave. A beautiful head was lowered beside the head of the bandit.

"Good girl," said The Red Devil. "Good old Meg. If you could understand him, you'd laugh along with me . . . and a pile louder."

"What at horse!" exclaimed Charlie Mark. "What a marvelous horse! My friend, you live up here like a king. Everything you see is yours, if you want it. You drop down out of the mountains like an eagle out of the sky, and take the

72

thing you desire. Then you turn around and scoot back up here and dissolve . . . drop out of sight."

"Maybe," said The Red Devil, "you'd like to change places with me?"

"Maybe!"

"I been seeing it in your eyes," the bandit said. "Well, you might fit in with the job a pile better than I do. Would you give up your home and live this sort of a life?"

"Why not?" asked Charlie Mark. "Why not? The old man could get along without me. Little he cares. So could the girl get along without me."

"Your father and your sweetheart, maybe you mean?" asked the robber.

"My father and sister. My father is Henry Mark." Why not tell the truth to this man who was about to die, so soon as the secret of the treasure was wormed out of him?

"You'd leave them?" asked the outlaw. "You'd leave them for the sake of the life I lead?"

"Isn't it good enough for you?"

For the first time The Red Devil seemed truly moved.

"It's good enough for me," he said. "I sure like the freedom of it. Sometimes I look off the mountain tops and down to the towns that I see in the valleys, and I pity the folks that live down there. I pity 'em because I feel like an eagle, and them down there . . . they're just field mice."

His color rose, and his eye flashed, but he changed almost at once. "That's only once in a while."

"Why'd you pick out the life, then?" demanded Charlie Mark.

"I was plumb forced into it," said the other. "I dunno why I waste words telling you this, but, low as you seem to be, son, I figure that you'd ought to be warned of the truth."

"Robber and sky pilot mixed together, eh?" asked Charlie Mark.

"Call it that if you want, but I was forced into this life, friend. I'll tell you how. My father killed a man by accident. A mob heard about it and thought it was murder. They came out and killed him. I got away from the house, but I plugged two of the boys that had helped at the killing. I thought they was dead, and started on my way. Well, they weren't dead, but I figured they were and I acted like my life was to pay, if I was caught. Before I'd gone a day's ride, I'd messed up the posse that rode after me, and I figured that I was gone, if ever I got in rifle range of a law-abiding citizen that knowed me. So I went on from one thing to another, and here I am. One thing I've done . . . I've never taken a cent except from crooks who didn't really deserve what they had. And even out of that coin, I've always sent back the money when I knew who it had been taken from."

"Look here!" broke in Charlie Mark. "D'you expect me to swallow that?"

"I don't think you will," replied Jim Curry, alias The Red Devil. "I don't think you will, but I'm going to tell you, just the same. That coin I took from Lang yesterday . . . d'you know why I stuck the stage up?"

"Because you wanted the stuff, I guess."

"*Bah!* The rancher had close to ten thousand, and Jake had a fat wad under the box."

"How do you learn those things?"

"I have friends, and the reason I have friends is because I play as square as I can. I heard that Lang had cleaned out a poor gent named Vincent, over the mountains. I made that special trip to get back the coin he'd taken. Every bill of it goes back to Vincent."

Charlie Mark burst into a tirade of laughter. "Do you expect me to believe that nonsense?"

"I expect you to believe this, at least," said Jim Curry solemnly. "The money you take at the point of a gun won't do you no good. It'll fill up your dreams."

"*Bah!*" exclaimed Charlie Mark. "I begin to see a chance. I begin to see a mighty good chance. Suppose I never turned you in. Suppose I shot you, my friend, The Red Devil, and left you here to rot in a grave, while I took your horse and slipped down to some of the towns? Why, they're wild with money. They have more than they know what to do with, and the first sight of the white horse and the red wig would make 'em throw up their hands. They wouldn't even begin to fight back. It would be a picnic, eh?"

He was striding up and down the cave by this time, full of the scheme, as it grew and expanded in his eager imagination.

"Does it sound as good as all that?" asked Jim Curry, studying the captor with a strange mingling of disgust and fascination.

"It does! The more I look at it, the better it seems." He was talking to The Red Devil simply because he had to talk to someone of the thoughts that were flowing through his brain.

"Hark to me a minute, will you?" demanded Jim Curry. "If you take up this job, partner, you'll curse yourself for it later on. You'll be lonely, and there ain't any demon in the world as bad as loneliness."

"Why should I have to be lonely?"

"Because you can't work this game if you have partners. It can't be done. Other gents have tried it. They've all been run down. It's the loneliness that kills 'em off, my boy. Look at the best of 'em. They go down. Why? Because they got to have noise around 'em. They got to have company to keep 'em from thinking about what they've done."

"And you don't?"

"I don't, thank goodness, because I've never done a killing in my life, sir."

Charlie Mark burst again into uproarious laughter.

"Do you really think that I'll believe that?"

"No, I don't think you will. I'm telling you, anyway."

"Go on. You make a pretty convincing liar, at that. You have the tune, I might say, even when you are a bit shaky on the words."

Jim Curry continued, unshaken by this badinage: "I tell you true. Of course they've saddled about a thousand killings on me. But they're wrong. I couldn't do it. I don't have to do it."

"Eh?"

"You don't have to do it," said Jim Curry, "if you can shoot straight enough and quick enough."

Back into the mind of Charlie Mark came the memory of how Lang had been shot cleanly through the arm at much risk to the outlaw, because, if the bullet had failed of this outside shot, a stream of lead from Lang's automatic must inevitably have ended the days of The Red Devil at once.

"You're good with a gun," he declared frankly. "Better than I could ever be."

"You'd improve, if you got into my shoes," said Curry. "A man can shoot pretty straight when he has to shoot straight. A lot of these desperadoes that break out of jails from time to time are ordinary, fair-to-middling shots, but, when they have to live by shooting straight, all at once they forget how to miss. I guess that's the straight of it."

"I understand," murmured Charlie Mark, listening with puckered brows.

"But the thing that makes it hard to get away with the life," said Curry, "is that the loneliness will get you. One of these days I'll look off the mountains and see the lights of some village and ride down for it, even knowing that I'll get a rope around my neck for taking the chance."

"Aye," said Charlie Mark. "But you don't know me. I'd never get lonely, if I got enough money and freedom and power out of it. Never!"

He spoke with great enthusiasm, enthusiasm so great that he did not notice that The Red Devil, while listening with great intentness, had slipped far down on the stone on which he had been sitting. Nor did Charlie Mark give heed to the fact that he was standing not four feet away from the other.

The first intimation that there might be danger in such close range came from a startling impact and a twinge of pain in his right hand. Then the gun, which had been kicked loose by the accurate toe of the robber, spun into the distance and exploded with a roar as it landed at some distance among the rocks of the cave.

Charlie Mark, with a shout of fear and surprise, sprang back, or tried to spring back, but, as he moved, the active legs of the other were wrapped around his, and he came crashing to the floor of the cave.

Still, the advantage was his, for he had struck on top, and beneath him was a man whose arms were bound tightly to his sides. But there seemed to be a slippery devil in Jim Curry. In an instant he had wriggled from beneath, and his fumbling hands, held short by the binding rope, had jerked the hunting knife out of Mark's belt, and now he held the deadly weapon close to the breast of the other.

"Steady up," he said in the ear of Mark, as they rolled over—Mark on top. "If you move, son, I'll give you the whole blade in your insides."

At the same time Charlie Mark felt the stinging point of the sharp knife through his shirt. Instantly he became still and rolled quietly over to the floor of the cave. If that knife had not been sunk at once into his flesh, it might be that the formidable fellow did not intend to kill. At least it was his only hope. With gleaming eyes he watched his conqueror, as the latter rose and severed the cords that bound him.

IX

The next move of the outlaw was to back up to the place where the gun that he kicked from the hands of Charlie Mark had fallen. He scooped it up, dropped it in into his own holster, and, disdaining with a fine indifference to keep his man covered, advanced upon Charlie Mark.

"Get up," he said coldly. "I don't remember asking you to lie down there."

Charlie, moving cautiously, for fear that a sudden motion might bring the gun snapping out of the holster, sat up and then rose to his feet.

"I guess I've told you true about one thing," said The Red Devil. "I don't kill unless I have to, and I haven't had to yet. Stand back . . . away from those guns . . . that's all I ask. But I warn you now, partner, that, if you make one move that I don't like, I'll be plumb tempted to send a slug through you. Understand, my boy?"

"Sure," replied Charlie Mark, sauntering to the far side of the cave, where he leaned against the wall.

"You're cool," said Jim Curry, watching attentively. "Take you all in all, you're about as cool a one as I ever seen."

"Thanks," said Charlie Mark.

"Don't thank me," answered the other, "because I didn't mean it that way."

So saying, he turned to the fire, presenting his back to the other as he did so, and heaped some more wood on it. There was a single twitch of the muscles of Charlie Mark. Was the robber doing this to tempt him? At least it was maddening to think that he should be held so lightly. In fact, he was still quivering with indignation, remembering with what ease The Red Devil had deprived him of his weapon and made him helpless. Yet he controlled the almost overmastering impulse to spring at the back of the outlaw. When Jim Curry turned from the brightened fire, he nodded almost amiably at his captive.

"You got a steady nerve and a cool head," he complimented Charlie Mark. "I'm only sorry that you ain't a man, a real man, to use it the right way."

"Thanks," said Charlie Mark. "I'll manage things my own way and get along as well as I can."

The outlaw smiled. Apparently he was greatly pleased by this indomitable steadiness.

"A gent with a nerve like yours," he said, "could be. . . ." Here he paused and continued on another tack. "Whatever come into your head a while back that you'd like to have my place?"

"I meant it then," said Charlie Mark, "and I mean it now."

Jim Curry smiled again and shook his head, as one bewildered. Then he leaned, still apparently thinking, and scooped up a small package that had fallen to the ground.

"You see this?" he asked.

"Well?"

"That's the money I got out of the lining of Lang's coat. It's going back to the gent that has the best right to it . . . old Vincent, who worked his heart out getting what I have here in my hand."

"Great guns," said Charlie Mark, "and I could have had it just by picking it up. How much is in it?"

"Twenty-one thousand nine hundred and eighty-five. I counted it pretty careful, but I didn't think that the old man had as much as this."

"Twenty-one thousand!" Charlie Mark whistled. "That's a neat haul. You won't have to work much for a few months, eh?"

"You don't think I'll send it back?"

Charlie Mark grinned sardonically, and Curry, eying him with pity and contempt, bestowed the package in an inner pocket and made no answer. That silence was more convincing to Charlie Mark than a thousand hours of talk. All at once he felt strangely inferior to the outlaw, and the sense of inferiority goaded him sharply.

"What's up now?" he asked.

"You've messed things up for me now," said Curry gloomily. "I've been pretty snug here, but, now that you've found the place out, I've got to leave."

"You're going to turn me loose, I suppose," answered Charlie Mark. "You're going to turn me loose in spite of what I said I was going to do to you?" But in spite of his sneer, he was white-lipped with fear and hope.

Jim Curry gave vent to a burst of uncontrollable disgust. "D'you think I can kill you out of hand? A minute ago, when I turned my back on you, I admit that I was sort of hoping that you'd tackle me, and then I'd've finished you . . . maybe. It was sure a temptation." He sighed. "But that's over. And now . . . but let's get back to what you we're talking about. D'you know, Mark, that, if you were to put on that red wig and ride that white horse, you could play my part about as well as I play it?"

"What of that?"

"Suppose I was to step out and let you step in?"

"You're laughing at me!"

"Laughing at you? You fool, I'm simply seeing if you'd really throw yourself away."

"Throw myself away?" Charlie Mark laughed comfortably. "Don't worry about that, son. As soon as I had a fat wallet, I'd be away where you dig your gold with a pack of cards."

The Red Devil snapped his fingers suddenly.

"Gambler," he muttered. "I should have guessed it. I'm losing my eyes. You'd take the place, then?"

"Try me!"

"And let me get out from under? You'd show yourself on the white horse somewhere in the next couple of days, so that I could show up a couple of hundred miles away and you'd be my alibi?"

"I'd be acting quick, once I got into your shoes. I wouldn't let any grass grow under my feet, I can tell you."

The outlaw rolled a cigarette and smoked it with huge, lung-filling, meditative puffs. "I guess you wouldn't," he muttered. "If I simply walk out, and nobody takes up the part, I'll be nabbed. Too many folks have seen me . . . too many of 'em have heard me talk. But if somebody else was cavorting around on the white horse while I. . . ." He stopped short, drawing a great breath. "Mark," he said, "you can have the outfit, if you want it. Maybe I'm wrong for letting you throw yourself away, but I figure that you're the kind that would do it sooner or later, anyhow."

Charlie Mark shrugged his shoulder, studying the face of his companion with the most intense interest.

Then Curry stepped back and whistled softly, a sound that brought the white mare instantly from the depths of the darkness in the cave.

She was a most exquisite creature. Never in his life had Charlie Mark seen such a horse. She was not entirely white, but finished off with dark points on each foot and at the muzzle, and between her eyes, exactly in the center of the broad, intelligent forehead, there was a black splotch. This was that famous Meg, whose speed had never yet been matched in the mountains.

"Honey," the tall outlaw was saying softly to the mare, "it sure goes hard for you and me to take a split trail, with you going one way, me going another way. But there ain't anything else to do, I guess." He turned suddenly upon Charlie Mark. "Friend," he said, "if I was ever to hear about you mistreating this horse, they ain't space enough in these here mountains for you to run away in."

"D'you mean," exclaimed Charlie Mark, "that you're going to give me a flyer at this game?"

"Yep," said Curry gravely. "If you think it's a game, I give you a chance at it, and you're sure welcome."

A great deal may pass in a short time through the mind of a man who is accustomed to make decisions concerning life and death in the space of time it takes him to draw his revolver out of its holster.

"Only one thing I ask of you," Curry said after a moment of further consideration. "How are you with horseflesh?"

"My worst enemy has to admit that I deal kindly with them," said Charlie Mark. "I suppose you worry about the mare. I'll be good to her."

"Will, you?" murmured the outlaw wistfully. "Honest? But if you ain't, friend, and, if I get sight of it or word of it, I'll come calling on you, and kill you, Mark, with no more on my soul than if I killed a mad dog. Her and me? Why, we've been through life and death together."

X

It was hardly an hour later that Charlie Mark sat on the back of the white mare for the first time and jogged her out of the cave and onto the hillside. He had obeyed all the final instructions of Curry for placing the great stone across the entrance to the cave, a thing that was easily done by the use of some thick sticks by way of levers, and now he rode Meg across the hills and rejoiced in the manner of her going. For she was finer than anything he had ever bestrode. She had not the dazzling speed in a straightaway that characterizes the thoroughbred. Charlie Mark had ridden clean-bred horses in plenty in the East. But Meg had an easy grace of movement such as he had never known. Soon he discovered that her gait was not only frictionless in seeming, but apparently untiring to her.

Uphill and downhill she maintained the same steady pace.

It was not hard to discover that this was the road pace taught her by her last master. Charlie Mark marveled at this average speed. If she had not the dazzling foot for a single burst, she certainly more than made up for it by her endurance. What hunter could have kept up with her in a twenty-mile test across all manner of mountain land? She had the surety of a cat. She seemed to have eyes in her feet, reading the nature of the soil or rock beneath her, never so much as starting a pebble rolling when she careered down a steep mountainside. No wonder that The Red Devil had parted from his mare with bitterness of heart.

As for Charlie Mark, he finally drew rein on the crest of a hill that overlooked two towns in the plain below. Both were unknown to him, and both, from the place where he sat the saddle, were merely so many dots of light against the darkness. And yet those dots of light meant the dwellings of men, and where the dwellings of men were, were the fortunes of men, dollars and cents. Charlie Mark rubbed his hands and settled his hat more firmly on his head, for it was loose on the mass of hair in the red wig. Horse, wig, mask, he had taken the outfit of The Red Devil to himself entirely. It was almost like taking a guarantee against punishment for sin. Below him lay the world. Let him do what he chose; he could never be found out.

He touched Meg with his heel. She was away at once and down the slope, heading by her own choice for the village on the right. So be it. Hers was the volition, felt Charlie Mark, that was launching the avalanche of destruction on the heads below.

If he had been an old hand, he would never have dreamed of taking that course, or, indeed, any other that led to plunder so near the home cave. But Charlie Mark was in no mood to observe caution. He was on a horse that, according to The Red Devil and the passengers in the stage-coach, could not be overtaken by any animal in the mountains. And, besides, before leaving the cave, Charlie had tried the revolver and found that his hand had by no means lost all of its old cunning. That skill, reinforced by the paralyzing effect of the reputation of The Red Devil, ought surely to make him invincible. And Charlie Mark threw back his head and broke into a song.

Stopping that song only when the lights grew large before him, he skirted down the back of the town and brought Meg to a halt and considered the work before him, while the mare turned her head in perfect silence, as if she understood that it would be fatal to betray their presence by any stir of foot or voice.

Charlie Mark studied the backs of the houses.

They were dark and blank to him. What meaning, after all, had they? Was he not a fool to have come down here, without first laying out a map for the campaign of looting? For instance, where was the post office, and where in the post office was the safe? And, even if he knew where the safe was, where was his soup for blowing the door off the safe?

Reflection told him that he had been very foolish indeed to make this night excursion. But, in the meantime, it would do no harm to have a look into one or two of the lighted windows, which peered back at him through screening trees.

Dismounting, he left Meg standing and went off to investigate. The first window into which he glanced showed him a kitchen scene, with the woman of the house busily engaged in scouring pans. The second window exposed a child's bedroom, with a freckle-faced youngster digging his knuckles into his forehead in the intensity of his efforts to get at the heart of the arithmetic problem for next day's school. But the third window showed at least an early glimpse of promise. It gave to his view, as he slipped up onto the rear of the verandah and came to the window, a room filled with blue mist and curling wisps of smoke. In the center was a round table, and about the table sat five men in their shirt sleeves, in the very act of leaning forward to view the results of a call. The winner of the hand drew in a formidable stack of chips, and the loser, who had apparently bucked up the game very high, shoved a $20 bill at the banker for more chips. The latter opened to the curious and interested eye of Charlie Mark a drawer literally filled with a tangle and drift of greenbacks. He deposited the $20, drew out a little stack of chips, and closed the treasure again. Charlie Mark moistened his dry lips with his tongue.

Here was a haul of indefinite size. There might be $10,000 in that drawer, but probably there was not $1,000. Should he risk his life to take $1,000? Certainly not, if he had been in the East. But here in the West, armed with a name, a rôle, and a past that were worth ten armed men obeying his orders, he could afford to risk himself cheaply.

The open window was close to the porch and he had only to draw his gun, duck his head, and step in. At once he was in the bluish mist of smoke, covering the company with his Colt. And yet they were so intent on their game that not a head had turned.

For an instant a great impulse rose in him to sweep off his mask before he had been observed, shove his revolver back in the holster, and simply ask to sit in at the game. Before he could obey that last-minute impulse, however, an eye flashed up at him, there was a grunt of horror, and, without the necessity of speaking a single word, he suddenly found himself confronted by five tall men, each one with his quivering hands above his head.

Someone muttered: "The Red Devil."

That whisper was exceedingly pleasant to Charlie Mark.

"Get back against the wall!" he commanded harshly.

Instantly they obeyed and faded back through the mist, until their shoulders came flat against the wall. Charlie Mark stepped to the table, jerked out the drawer, dumped the contents on the table, and then transferred them into his coat pocket, sweeping in the wrinkled bills, by sense of touch rather than sight, and noting all the time that terror froze the others, so that they dared not even express regret with a glance. Certainly the repute of The Red Devil was strong in Peterville.

While he backed toward the window, a feeling that was almost kindness arose in Charlie Mark. It had been all so easy, so ridiculously easy. The great marvel was that more men had not taken to this or a similar game. And then, as he continued his backward motion, it seemed to Charlie that a peculiar meaning came in the eyes that were staring at him. They seemed suddenly interested in something behind and beyond him, and a tense suspense drew their lips to straight lines.

Like a flash the meaning dawned in the mind

of Charlie Mark. He did not pause to question. He whirled in his tracks and bolted not for the window behind him, but for the door just to one side of it. There was a roar of two guns from the window, and from the corner of his eye he saw the two men who had stolen up to the window from the outside on the verandah. From the other corner he saw the five men who he had held up jump into action and reach for guns.

He was through the door before he could see more. He whirled down a narrow hall and, turning to the right, dashed the door open into the very face of one of the two men who had come up on the verandah behind him. The impact knocked the fellow back, but Charlie Mark, frightened to the point of desperation, did not trust that shock. He fired pointblank, saw the man crumple like a wet rag, and then leaped across the verandah to the ground beyond.

A gun roared to his right so close that the flash leaped at him like the dart of a snake's tongue. Charlie Mark whirled and shot almost carelessly before he was completely turned. The second man lurched sidewise and fell with a crash.

The house, at that moment, belched guns and men from every door and window, it seemed to the robber, and he sprinted desperately into the friendly darkness, with a rain of bullets following after him.

In another moment he was beside the mare.

As he sprang into the saddle, a yell ran and echoed through the town of Peterville: "The Red Devil's come! You can't foller his hoss. Wait and get together! Wait and get together!"

A sudden courage came hot in throat of Charlie Mark. Behind him lay two dead men. The double murderer threw back his head and sent a ringing shout of defiance into the darkness. Then Meg bore him away, as on the wings of the wind.

XI

In the town of Hampton, old Henry Mark seated himself in the chair outside the post office, which was also the verandah of the general store, the social and business and political center both of the town and the entire county. On this verandah he settled down, rubbing his fingers through his long white beard, very much in the manner of a man so intensely interested in what he read that he was unaware of the fact that his daughter was waiting for him. She held a fretting team of horses that danced in front of the buckboard, although soothed by her quiet voice and checked by her deft manipulation of the reins.

She saw his white eyebrows go up, then draw together in a tremendous frown. Truly it must be strange news and bad news, and Ruth Mark sighed, for her father, in his times of petulance, could be a very trying man indeed for his family.

At length, when he had finished, he sat for some time with the letter gripped in both hands, his eyes staring far away, with such an expression of helpless grief that her heart went out to him strongly. Then he rose, and, whereas his step was usually brisk, and his carriage erect, he now went with bowed head and trailing feet.

"It's Charlie," murmured the girl, recognizing the symptoms. "News from nobody else could affect him in that manner."

And she was not really surprised when he announced, as he came beside the rig: "It's Charlie, Ruth. It's Charlie, again."

"What's he done?"

Her father groaned as he answered: "He's changed his mind about coming out."

There was a faint exclamation of indignation from Ruth. She had never had any great patience with her adopted brother. For such was the position of Charlie in the Mark family. Henry Mark and his wife, vainly awaiting the birth of a child, had finally adopted a homeless child, only to have a daughter born to them five years later. Yet a child of their own could have been no more dear to them than was Charlie. And especially was this true with the father. Ruth herself meant less to him than did the boy. And she, resenting this a little, had grown to detest Charlie for his utterly mercenary and heartless character. He showed sufficient affection to win a large quantity of spending money from Henry Mark, but there his love for his family ended, and, as for Ruth, she well knew that he hated and suspected her for the insight that had read through the meanness of his nature.

"But you told him, I thought," exclaimed the girl, "that you wanted him definitely to help take charge on the ranch?"

"I told him all of that and a pile more, besides. He's spending too much money out there in the East, Ruth. Not that I grudge him what he needs, but too much money for a young man is like too much candy for babies. They don't grow healthy on it. And Charlie has to walk straight from now on."

"Does he know that is what you intend?"

"He ought to guess it from the last letter I wrote to him."

A storm of angry accusation rose to her lips, a storm that she held back as well as she could, knowing by old experience that it did not pay to speak against her adopted brother.

"He says he's changed his mind," went on her father. "He's going to go up north and take a vacation."

"What has he been doing ever since he went East except take a vacation?"

"You're too hard on him, Ruth. He means well. I'm sure of that. But he has queer, flighty ways, that's all. I guess he wants to take one more fling at being a free man, as he calls it, before he comes out and settles down on the ranch. Well, let him go, only it's a bit hard on me." Slowly he continued: "We'll hitch up the team and sit down in the dining room for a while. I want to sort of get my wind after being hit by surprise this way."

She assented with a nod and, letting the horses trot to the hitching rack, swung with agile ease out of the seat and down to the road, carrying two halters. With these she tethered the horses and turned back to her father. Arm in arm they went back toward the conglomerate store hotel, and she knew, by the manner in which her father walked, that, had she been a man, he would have leaned heavily on her for support. Indeed that was the great, the crying regret of her life—that she was not a man. She could ride and shoot and throw a rope as well as the next one. She could have taken the place of a cowpuncher and ridden range or herd with any man. But she was only a girl, and therefore was a thing that men would rather pet and pamper because of her pretty face than treat as an equal.

Brooding on this perpetual and inescapable trouble, she went into the dining room with Henry Mark, and they sat down near the window. It was rather early for the noon meal, and hence the room was scantily occupied, saving for a tall lean man who sat in one corner eating his breakfast. He was distinguished by the sling in which he carried his right arm, and the clumsiness of his efforts to manage his fork with this left hand. Henry Mark at once forgot his own woes to talk about the other.

Leaning across the table toward his daughter, he whispered: "That's Lang."

"Really? The man The Red Devil held up?"

"That's the one. And he had the nerve to up and blaze away at the scoundrel. He didn't quite succeed in nailing his man, but Jake, the stage driver, says that it was the closest call a gent ever come to."

"But why didn't The Red Devil kill him, if he's such a terrible man?"

"Nobody can work out the ways of The Red Devil," said her father. "Some say that he's a pretty decent sort of a gent in some ways . . . others say that he's a murderer by nature, but just holds himself in for reasons of policy. I dunno. They tell a lot of hard things about him, and, if one half of them are true, he's a bad one, the worst that ever lived."

She listened negligently, for her mind had left the victim of the stage robber and gone back to her own affairs. They ordered their meal, and by the time the food appeared, the dining room was rapidly filling, for the hour of noon had come. And men in the West eat punctually, growing hungry by the clock, as it were.

Henry Mark reverted to the trouble with Charles Mark, and in talk of the dreariest nature they spent half of their dinner time. An interruption came violently and without warning.

There was a loud scraping of a chair pushed back. The tall form of Lang sprang to his feet, and, in a voice shaken crazily by rage, he called: "D'you folks in Hampton stand for this sort of thing?" As he spoke, he pointed with a long left arm to a man who was at that moment giving his order to the waiter. All eyes were turned at once in that direction. "D'you let 'em hold up stages on the road, and then come in and sit down and eat with you?"

"What's biting you?" asked the man who was being pointed out, and he was no other than Jim Curry.

"It's his voice," said Lang. "I'd know him in a million. I know him by his way and his build, and what he does with his hands, but mostly by that voice and them eyes. When you've seen an eye behind a gun, you ain't apt to forget soon what it looks like, and I tell you, even if he ain't got red hair . . . can't wigs be put on and put off? . . . that's The Red Devil!"

The name burst like a bomb on the dining room.

"Get him," said Lang. "Don't let him get away. He's got twenty-one thousand dollars that he lifted off of me. He's got that money, and I'll give a thousand of it to the gent that drops him for me."

"You fool," began Jim Curry, turning carelessly in his chair.

"Hands up," shouted Lang, "or I'll drill you clean!"

As he spoke, a lone revolver was conjured into his left hand, and with it he covered Curry.

"Gents," said Jim Curry rising, "is this gent crazy, or is he . . . ?"

"Hands up," said Lang.

"Is he crazy?" asked Curry, turning calmly to the amazed, nervous crowd.

"Look out!" cried half a dozen voices. "He's going to shoot!"

And, as they spoke, the gun spurted fire from the hand of Lang.

Jim Curry clapped his hands to his thigh, spun halfway around, and then, with admirable coolness, caught the back of a chair and lowered himself into it.

"Somebody get some cloth for bandages," Curry directed steadily. "And somebody else grab that infernal idiot . . . or I'll kill him, even if he only has one hand."

His coolness abashed Lang, and it did something more important, it won two-thirds of the way to his side the crowd of spectators. In a moment they were around him. None too gently Lang was thrust away, and Jim was carried tenderly out of the room and deposited on a leather-seated divan in the room that served as a lobby and office for the hotel.

There the leg was bared, washed, and bandaged, the whole work being completed before the doctor arrived, accompanied by the sheriff.

"What's this about shooting?" asked the sheriff. He made his way to the side of Curry and looked down at him. "Who did this?"

"A gent that says I'm The Red Devil," answered Jim. "That long fellow over there."

The sheriff whirled on his heel. "Who says that? What fool says that?" he asked. "Why, you idiot, don't you know the wire over to the telegraph office has been humming for the last ten minutes with a story about how The Red Devil dropped down into Peterville this morning, early, got away with a bunch of swag, and killed Joe Thomas and Hank McGuire, while he was getting away?"

"It can't be right," declared Lang, positively staggering with astonishment.

There was a groan from Jim Curry.

"It's the leg," he answered, when someone inquired what had hurt him. And he asked: "Two men, Sheriff? Did The Red Devil kill two men?"

"Two men," said the sheriff, "and it was The Red Devil, all right. He was riding Meg, and he had the same crop of red hair sticking out under the brim of his hat. Lang, you can trot along to the lockup with me and think this over. Partner, what's your name?"

"Jim," said Curry, "is the name I go by."

"Well, Jim," said the sheriff kindly, "we'll see that you're taken care of. Got any money?"

Jim Curry fumbled at a package in his pocket that contained twenty-one thousand and some odd dollars. But all of that must go to another man. "No," he said truthfully enough, "I haven't any money but some small change."

"All right," began the sheriff.

But here the tall, white-headed form of Henry Mark broke through the circle around the wounded man.

"Sheriff," he said, "I got lots of room out to my house. If he's well enough, I'll take him out today. I been talking to my girl about him, and, she and me agree that he's played the coolest game we've ever seen. Suppose he'd been The Red Devil . . . don't you think he would have filled Lang full of lead? But what he really is, is a square gent who wouldn't fight back against a crippled man like Lang. Sheriff, let me take him along."

"Have your own way," said the sheriff, glad that the public burden had been assumed by one capable pair of shoulders. "Have your own way, Mark."

Jim Curry had been lying still, with his eyes

half closed and his face puckered up. Now his eyes widened suddenly.

"What name?" he asked.

"Henry Mark," said that kindly rancher. "You look to me, son. I'll take care of you. You sure played man in not diving for your guns."

But here Jim Curry fell back on the seat.

"He rides down and kills two men . . . and here I am going into his own home. They's some kind of fate behind this exchange."

The bystanders looked blankly at one another.

"Hush," said Ruth Mark very softly, raising her hand and cutting short the volley of astonished comment that began. "Don't speak. There mustn't be much noise. Poor fellow, the fever has begun already, and he's delirious. Let me take charge of him."

And the wretched Jim Curry opened his eyes, and stared up at her with a strange, burning glance.

"I ain't worthy of a touch of your hand," he said.

JIM CURRY'S TEST

I

Even before Little Billy would fight with hard, freckled fists, he was called by that half-affectionate, half-contemptuous diminutive. He had not yet reached the emerging age, but he was not more than a year short of it. In fact, Billy was eleven, which, as everyone knows, is the last year of the real childhood of a boy who lives between the Rockies and the Sierras. At twelve he enters his time of apprenticeship. This is largely because the work of the cowpuncher requires more skill than strength, no matter how contrary to this the general opinion may be. It requires endurance to stick on the back of a horse, to be sure, but endurance and muscle are not the same. And as for throwing a rope and a steer, everyone who has done it will agree that the knack is of greater value than the brawn of a Hercules impressed for the job.

In the last year of childhood, then, was Little Billy, straight as a wand and of proportions not much more sturdy, brown of skin save where the brown was relieved with bright-red freckles, and with a head of windy hair sun-faded to a nondescript hue. The one colorful thing about his face, indeed, was the pair of intensely blue, intensely alive eyes.

He was laughing and dancing from foot to foot in his excitement as Ruth Mark looked out from the window and noted him. She remembered how he had first been brought from the town to the ranch by her great-hearted father. There was no explanation about his parenthood. And that was sufficient to assure Ruth that Henry Mark had found a forlorn orphan and had determined to give the boy a home. He had grown into a strange, impish little chap, under-size—and over-bright, she had always thought. He saw through grownups as a ray of sunshine looks through clear ice. He saw through her and made her uneasy before him. He saw through Henry Mark with such ease that the rancher hesitated, and never quite had made up his mind to adopt the waif as he had adopted Charlie, that other waif of an older day, ungrateful wanderer now.

Indeed, there was something terrible about the child. All persons felt his impish cleverness and insight. In the bunkhouse the cowpunchers dreaded him like a blight. He was a cross between a child and a man. He had the size of a child and a few of a child's ways. For the rest, he could ride like a man, handle his own pet .32-caliber revolver far better than most experts could handle a .45, and throw a knife with the uncanny skill of an Italian master. In general his list of war-like accomplishments read like those of some hero of the frontier, where a man learned to fight well nigh before he learned to walk.

No wonder, then, that Ruth Mark, for all her kindness of heart, eyed the child with a mixture of admiration, wonder, and fear, while Little Billy danced from one bare foot to the other in the dust, and poised the rubber ball lightly in his raised right hand.

She knew by the first glance who he was aiming that ball at. As clearly as in a mirror, the face of Jim was imagined. For no one else would Little Billy have exhibited a tithe of this interest, this fear, as though he at whom he was about to cast the ball might dart in inescapable pursuit and work a great revenge. The expression of the impish little chap was the expression of a monkey tormenting a lion, and from a distance that he was not quite certain was secure.

She ran her glance to the left, by dint of pressing her face close to the glass of the window, and there, with his back against an angle of the house, stood Jim himself. And as always when she glanced at him, her heart jumped a little. It had jumped when she first saw him in the hotel not so very many days before—that time when the tall man, Lang, had jumped up, accused Jim of being The Red Devil, and shot him through the thigh. And ever since Henry Mark brought the stranger home to be healed, his daughter had felt that strange, breathless, painful interest in the man who announced no name except Jim. Plain Jim he was, and had been ever since he arrived, and as to his past his lips were locked. Now he stood with his back to the wall of the house, and his brown hands dropped carelessly into his trouser pockets. With bored indifference he regarded the sparkling face of the boy opposite him.

The hard rubber ball was raised, the poising arm of the boy quivered—suddenly it was hurled with all his might, dissolving into a streak of light that flashed straight at the head of Jim. The latter waited until he thought the ball had well nigh struck him and then, with a movement of such cat-like speed and grace combined that Ruth could hardly follow it, he was out of the way. There was not the slightest bit of extra and unneeded effort in his side-step. He moved only far enough to allow the ball to whir past his very cheek, and it rebounded with a *thud* from the solid wall and back to the hands of the child.

"Pretty slow," Jim said quietly. "Darnation slow, son, I'd call that. If you can't learn to do a pile better, you'll never be no account with your gun work. I'd give up that gun work if I was you."

Ruth saw the boy flush to the roots of his hair. He fairly trembled with shame and indignation. From the first moment he laid eyes on Jim, he had made the stranger his hero. Hours and hours he had been content to sit by the bedside of the tall man and fix half-frightened, half-idolatrous eyes upon him.

"I would have hit you easy," he declared now, "if it hadn't been that the damned. . . ."

"Hush up," cautioned Jim, working his shoulders into a more comfortable position against the board behind him. "You ain't big enough to start cussing like that."

"Don't I hear you cuss every day?"

"Sure you do. But I'm studying your ways mighty careful, Billy, and before long I expect I'll be out of the habit. Cussing don't do no good. It don't help you none, and it don't hurt the thing you cuss at none. I want you to lay off that habit."

"Hmm," murmured the child thoughtfully. "Maybe I'd better. But you think I'm pretty slow, Jim?"

"Terrible. Never saw worse. If . . ."—here the ball flashed again from the hand of Little Billy, but the speaker, without hesitating over a single word, drifted out of the path with another of those incredibly rapid and smooth side-steps— "you was to take time and practice doing things, you might get pretty fair."

"Practice? Don't I practice a pile?"

"Practice?" The tall man chuckled. "Why, son, you don't know what it means. There ain't nothing worth doing that you don't have to practice at. Look at the way you come running along with that ball, all ready to soak somebody with it, and jest nacherally expecting that I'd stand still and let myself get soaked." He shook his head, smiling. "What's nine-tenths of winning a fight, Little Billy? It's keeping from getting hit. You're young. You got time to learn. But you got to practice hard. The way to win a fight is not to get hit by the other gent."

The boy listened with eyes and mouth agape. "You practice dodging a lot, Jim, I guess."

"Fair to middling lot. Boxing is the best practice. You got to get your hands and your feet moving all the time in that game. I ain't got the build or the weight for it. But I got the speed out of practice. I ain't got the shoulder drive to knock the ribs out of the other gent . . . but, if I ain't hurting him much, you can lay to it that he most likely ain't hitting me at all."

There was an exclamation of delighted amazement from the boy. "Can anybody lick you, Jim?" he asked. "Can anybody beat you at anything?"

"Sure," responded Jim instantly. "A pile of gents can beat me all hollow. The worst fool in the world can beat the best man in it, if he gets the break. Suppose I was to get into a fight and try to pull my gun, and suppose that gun was to stick a little. Well, Billy, any halfway decent gun-fighter ain't more than a little part of a second slower than the fastest at getting out his gun and pulling the trigger . . . and no matter if I was the king of 'em all, the worst fool could beat me, if I was to have a bit of bad luck and the gun was to bind against the leather."

"What good is it, then?" exclaimed the boy, who had listened to the gospel of "practice makes perfect" with the utmost devout attention. "What good is it to practice all the time? Luck might beat you."

"I'll tell you why it's good to practice. The best reason is . . . so's you won't have to fight."

"What?"

The girl at the window smiled and pressed her face closer to the glass until her nose was a white smudge behind it. She was beginning to see the reason behind this lesson in gunfighting.

"Sure," went on Jim complacently. "A gent that knows how to handle his gun fine never has to lay a hand on it. Why? Because what he can do will be knowed pretty quick without him saying a word about it. And then folks let him alone, you can bet."

"But . . . ," protested Little Billy gloomily.

"What you want to do," said Jim, chuckling, "is to get good with a gun, and then go out and shoot somebody up when you're a mite older. Eh?"

"Well," said the freckle-faced youngster, "I sure don't aim to take water from nobody."

"Nope, you want to get lightning fast, and then

go up ag'in' a gent that ain't wasted a couple of hours a day on gun play. Then you wouldn't be in a fight. You'd be doing a murder. Just the same's I'd be doing a murder, now, if I was to go after you. Understand?"

The point in ethics slowly penetrated to the savage mind of the child. He looked at Jim with a mixture of awe and disappointment.

"And now," said Jim, "you've had two cracks at me with a ball that would sting like sixty if it ever landed. What am I going to do to get back at you?"

"I dunno," said the boy. "I didn't think about that."

"Well," said Jim, "I guess you don't need nothing more done to you . . . because somebody's been looking and seen how you couldn't hit me."

Ruth Mark exclaimed in shame and surprise. He must have seen her from the back of his head, it seemed. She stepped out of view behind the wall and stood there, wondering why her face was so hot, and why her nerves tingled so, and why she was smiling so foolishly—all because she had been espied playing the part of a most innocent eavesdropper. She decided for the twentieth time that there was a certain something about this Jim.

II

The sheriff was not above doing duty as keeper also in the Hampton jail. It cut down expenses when there was no one inside the bars, which happened fifty percent of the time, and, when a prisoner was lodged there, anyone could be entrusted with the task of guarding him. The up-to-date steel and concrete of the Hampton jail was its own best security. Now Sheriff Nance went with the jingling keys and unlocked the door of the only cell that was occupied. He gestured to a tall, gaunt man sitting disconsolately on a cot with his skinny arms wrapped about his skinnier knees.

"Well," asked the prisoner without looking up, "ain't you going to get out and leave me be, if I can't get no justice done in this town?"

"Stand up," said the sheriff, by whose voice it might be guessed that he was not on the best of terms with the tall man. "Come on out here. I'm through with you."

"I sure wish you was, son."

"I am, Lang. Come on out. We're all through with you. That fool out at Henry Mark's place ain't going to prosecute you none, and I ain't going to bother hounding you for a while for breaking the peace. Crimes like that . . . I mostly don't bother none with. Anyway, he's turning you loose, and you can thank your lucky stars for it. I rode out to see him yesterday. 'Jim,' says I, 'what you going to do? When you going to lay the charge, now that you're all healed up? I can't hold him no more for vagrancy.'

"'Let him go,' says Jim to me. 'Let him just go. Him being in jail ain't going to put no fat on my ribs, I guess.'"

"He's afraid that, if I hang around these parts, in jail or out, the truth will get circulated about him," asserted Lang. "That's what's biting him."

The sheriff laughed scornfully, but so great was his indignation that the scorn presently changed to anger and the laughter to a growl.

"You still keeping up that fool talk about Jim being The Red Devil?" he asked.

"I'm sure doing it," persisted Lang through his teeth.

"That's the most out-beatingest fool talk I ever heard," said the sheriff. "Don't you know that The Red Devil has been hoofing it around promiscuous and worse'n ever since you was locked up and this Jim gent lying flat on his back?"

"I dunno nothing about that," declared Lang, shaking his bullet head with irritating firmness of purpose. "All I know is that the voice and the eyes behind the gun that held up the stage the other day was the voice and the eyes of this gent that calls himself plain Jim. By the way, ain't nobody curious to find out what his other name might be?"

"Better men than you or me," said the sheriff solemnly, "have gone about and lived plumb comfortable in this part of the country, and done it all packing around only one name with 'em. I guess this Jim can do the same. They say that the Mark family likes him fine."

"He's turned the girl's head," said Lang, scowling. "The skunk is handsome enough to do that, and I ain't denying it."

The sheriff exploded. "You've said about enough," he declared. "Here's a gent that you say you seen behind a mask. He ain't got red hair, and yet you say that, with different hair and in spite of the mask, you recognize him by his voice and his eyes. Well, Lang, that can't be done. And I tell you what I and all the rest of the folks in this neck of the woods think . . . they think that you're lucky not to be sent up by Jim for what you done . . . shooting him down without giving him . . . no chance to make a play. Why, even a snake wouldn't act that way."

Lang made no audible protest against this outburst of abuse, but his upper lip writhed silently back from long, dog-sharp teeth, and his eyes glinted at the sheriff from the corner of the sockets. Truly it was an evil look, and the sheriff felt a chill chase up and down his spine.

"You go your way, and I'll go my way," said Lang. "But the time's going to come, and you mark my word for it, when I'll prove that it was this gent you call Jim that held up the stage and got my twenty-one thousand dollars, and then come straight on into Hampton and trusted that he wouldn't be recognized because of his mask."

"And how come The Red Devil still to be riding around the country killing gents and taking their coin?" said the sheriff, forcing himself to be calm of voice.

"I dunno," muttered Lang, bending his head while his face darkened with thought. "Maybe they was always two of 'em, and the taking of one wouldn't stop the other."

"Two with red hair . . . two white Megs for 'em to ride on?"

This piling up of the impossibilities made Lang shake his head and desist from argument. "Keep right on your own way," he said gloomily. "You'll sure cuss yourself for it someday. You'll sure cuss yourself."

The sheriff had led the way into his office in the front of the jail. Now he strode to the wall and jerked down a small, framed photograph, three inches by four. He thrust it into the hand of Lang.

"Take this along with you," he said fiercely. "When you first got to talking with me, I went out to the Mark place with my Kodak, and I took

116

a snapshot of Jim and brought it back and developed it and hung it up here. And ever since then I've been asking gents if they ever heard of him or anything bad about him. And not one of them can say that they have. Now you take the picture, son, and go along and see how many bad things they'll say about Jim."

"And didn't it strike you queer," muttered Lang, "that none of the gents you talked to had ever seen him? Where'd he come from, then? Did he drop down out of the clouds?"

This phase of the matter had apparently not come to the attention of the worthy sheriff. Now he stared uneasily at Lang for a moment, and even seemed on the verge of asking that the photograph be restored to him for further official inquiry about the original. But Lang, feeling that he had turned the tide of the conversation and planted a strong doubt in the mind of the sheriff, turned on his heel and left the jail before another word could be spoken to him.

He turned down the street to the hotel, and there he took a chair on the verandah, tilted it back against the wall of the building, and cast a casual observation over those who were coming in and filing out. He was amazed to find that he had no real resentment against the sheriff and the other people of the town for his long confinement. His brain was wholly occupied with the problem of how he could prove the guilt of the

117

man he had shot down under suspicion of being the terrible Red Devil who had taken over $21,000 from him. It mattered not that that large sum of money had been obtained by Lang by criminal methods. It had once been his. He had been robbed of it and shot through the arm when he resisted robbery. And his whole soul rose into a rage when he remembered.

At least his actions in the town of Hampton had not gained him any very great popularity among the townsfolk. They came by him one after another without so much as a nod. A blank, cold stare was the utmost attention he drew, and he made up his mind that the practice of shooting men on sight and suspicion of unproved identity was by no means approved of. However, if they had been able to look into his past, they would have found more than this to frown at, and Lang let them go with a shrug of the shoulders. Their approval meant nothing in his young life.

He drew out the picture of Jim eventually, and fell into a brown study over the lean, handsome features, the rather over-bright eyes, the stern line of the mouth. So great was his preoccupation that he did not notice a stranger who sat down by his side until the latter uttered an exclamation.

"Partner, can I have a look at that?"

Lang jerked up his head and found beside him a squat-shouldered, gray-headed man who was staring at the picture in intense interest.

118

"Help yourself," answered Lang. "Look as long as you like. Know the gent?"

The other took the photograph eagerly and turned it so that the light fell from differing angles upon it.

"Know him?" he said at last. "I dunno, partner. Time changes a gent. And they's some folks that can hardly be told from others, even when they're standing shoulder to shoulder. But . . . ."

"Well . . . ?" urged Lang.

"Well, sir, why are you interested in that picture?"

Lang found two gray, steady eyes peering into his own. He hesitated, and then decided on frankness. "That's a gent," he said, "that I think has got a past that is as black as the ace of spades. I'm just packing his picture around trying to find out something about him."

"*Hmm,*" answered the stranger, melted into telling what he knew by this giving of a confidence. "Then I can tell you what I remember. Down south about six years ago we had a mix-up in my town with a family named Curry. It was kind of a hard thing for us, and it was sure a bad thing for the Curry family. Happened this way. Old Jim Curry was a shiftless sort. No harm in him, we thought, except that he liked fighting on general principles, and such as that ain't particular comfortable ones to have around in a town.

"One day we got word, sudden, that he'd murdered Dad Jackson, an old-timer everybody was pretty fond of, and then he had cleaned up the sheriff when the sheriff tried to put him in jail. Well, we had a posse on the road in fifteen minutes, found Jackson's dead body in ten minutes more, and wound up at the shack where Jim Curry and his son by the same name lived. We tried to get in. They wouldn't let us. We was masked, you see, and meant business . . . and the end of it was we forgot that the boy hadn't done nothing wrong, opened fire on the shack, and killed Jim Curry . . . as we found out later. Young Jim broke out, got to one of our hosses, and rode off . . . but he turned in the saddle and shot down a couple of gents.

"He got plumb away. But he figured that he'd killed two men, I guess, and he rode to beat fire through the mountains, stealing a new hoss when he tired out the one he was riding. Well, after he'd disappeared, we figured he was a killer and a hoss thief, but it turned out that both the gents that he dropped lived. And as for the hosses, the Curry place had enough stock on it to pay all claims, and more besides. But Jim Curry ain't never showed up down yonder. I guess he figures that he's wanted. And, at that, he is. The whole Ridgeley family would be after him because he broke Chet's leg, and Chet ain't been able to sit in a saddle since." Here the stranger paused.

"But it sounds to me," said Lang, "that a pile more was done ag'in' young Curry than he done ag'in' others."

"Maybe," agreed the other. "But I figure that the family was no good. His father was shiftless before him, and he was starting out the same way, concentrating mostly on gun play. You know? And this picture sure looks like a ringer for Jim Curry . . . the way he might look right today."

Lang sighed with pleasure as he put up the photograph. "Are you working around these parts?" he asked.

"Out to the Clark outfit."

"Good," murmured Lang. "That's handy. And suppose you don't say nothing about Jim Curry being in town."

"Sure I won't," answered the stranger, "because I ain't sure. I'd know if I seen his face . . . that's all."

"Maybe you'll see it one of these days," said Lang. "But not yet. I need more proof . . . a pile more proof. But I think, partner, that Jim Curry . . . if that's his name . . . is going to wish that you and me had never met up."

Lang rose from his chair and passed thoughtfully down the steps. In his heart there was something akin to a savage song of triumph. He had won in his first step, he felt. Other victories would follow, for by instinct he was certain—

utterly certain—that the man at the Mark place was Jim Curry, and that Jim Curry was The Red Devil.

III

It was only by chance that Jim and Little Billy saw him. They had walked farther than Jim intended, seeing that this was the first extended exercise he had taken since his wound had been received. And as a result the muscles of the left leg, which had received the bullet, had grown weak and lame, and he had come haltingly toward the Mark house with his left hand bearing heavily down on the shoulder of Little Billy. Little Billy winced more than once under the pressure, but he never complained verbally; he was weak with weariness as they came up the last rise and saw the house through the trees.

Under the shadow of those trees he halted abruptly, so abruptly that Jim nearly stumbled forward on his hands and knees.

"What's that yonder?" whispered Little Billy.

And he pointed straight up the side of the house and at the window of what had been the room of Charlie Mark, although it was now converted for the use of Jim. There, framed dimly in the window, was what appeared to be the form of a man, although very faintly sketched against the deeper blackness of the interior of the room by the hazy light of a thin young moon.

"Well?" asked Jim.

"D'you see him?" breathed the boy.

"No. I thought I did a minute ago, though."

"He's just stepped back into the room, and that's why you can't see him," asserted the boy.

"It's Henry Mark," suggested Jim. "He's been grieving a pile about Charlie, eh? Maybe he's up there sitting and thinking about Charlie."

"Listen," answered Little Billy. "Ain't that the governor singing downstairs?"

Large and true the voice of the governor floated out of a lower window of the house, a window across which the silhouette of Ruth Mark drifted a moment later.

"It's somebody, right enough," muttered Jim. "Who the devil could it be?"

"It sure is," said the boy, his voice quivering, and, in an impulse of fear, he clung suddenly to his companion's hand. In a moment he had mastered his fear, however, and he continued pointing to the left.

"Look yonder. Jim . . . Jim . . . it's The Red Devil that's come."

Barely distinguishable in the moon haze was the outline of a white horse standing among the trees.

"The Red Devil," repeated the child. "And that's his hoss . . . white Meg!"

There was a convulsive start in his companion. "Lord," muttered Jim. "I half believe it is. What's the fool come down here for?"

"What for? Murder," said the trembling boy. "Ain't that why he goes other places? Ain't that why he lives . . . just to kill gents and take their money?"

"Hush," said Jim. "Don't talk, Little Billy. I got to think."

And Little Billy was still as a mouse watched by a cat. His heart was hammering in fear for the safety of Ruth Mark and her father, alone in the house with the murderer—with nothing to protect them save two old Chinese servants who would not know one end of a gun from the other. It seemed obvious to Little Billy that the only thing to do was, first of all, to secure white Meg, the matchless horse, and then rush to the front of the house and call Henry Mark and his daughter out. But Jim had other ideas, and Jim could not be wrong. Billy worshiped his new-found hero with all his heart.

"You stay here," said Jim. "Stay right here and don't move. No, you better sit down here in the grass under the trees . . . and once you're there, don't budge, I tell you."

"You ain't going up there into the house alone?" pleaded the boy in a terrified whisper. "You ain't going up there all alone to kill The Red Devil, Jim? Not even you could do that . . . please!"

124

But Jim brushed him away. "Don't talk," he commanded.

"Well," said the boy, making the best of what seemed a very bad proposition, "what am I to do? Ain't I going to get a chance even to get white Meg?"

Jim hesitated, his breath coming hard and fast. Then he shook his head. "Not a hand on her," he said sadly. "She might raise the devil, if you come near her, son. She's a man-killer for fair."

With this last dreadful warning, which made Little Billy shrink against the trunk of the nearest tree, Jim vanished to the right, appeared again crossing the clearing of the house, and then was gone around the corner of the building.

He came in through the rear entrance of the house and stealthily mounted toward his room —which had formerly been the room of Charlie Mark. In the upper hall he crouched—almost flattened himself against the floor, where the ear catches most readily all the sounds of moving feet. But there was not a whisper.

He's learned his lessons fast, mused Jim to himself. *But then he was just nacherally born to the trade.*

He slipped on down the hall to the door of the room, his own movement, despite the hampering weakness of his wounded leg, as noiseless as the stalking of a cat. At the door he raised his hand, and, after listening again for a moment, he rapped twice or thrice very softly.

Still there was no sound from the room, and now he pushed the door an inch ajar. At that, there was a faint whispering sound in the darkness, a strange, light sound, although Jim recognized it perfectly. It was the *hiss* of a gun drawn rapidly out of the holster.

"It's me," whispered Jim loudly. "It's Jim Curry. Are you there, Charlie?"

There was a pause. Then came the light *creak* of a board.

"Well," said a voice that apparently despised whispering, because it ventured at once on a soft speaking tone, "what d'you want, Jim Curry?"

"I want to tell you, you three-ply fool, that the kid is downstairs under the trees, and that he's seen white Meg. What in thunder are you doing back here?"

The door was here swung softly back in the gloom. Through the darkness he vaguely made out the form of a man.

"I came back to look around," said the other. "I'm just amusing myself. Anything wrong with that?"

"Everything's wrong with it. If you got a thimbleful of brains, you'd ought to know it."

"I don't like that sort of talk," said the other savagely. "Keep your face shut if you can't talk decently to me."

There was a groan from Jim. "I'll talk anyway you want, only . . . get out of the house."

"Why?" persisted the other. "Isn't this my home? Haven't I a right to stay here?"

Jim groaned again. "Come across the hall," he said. "We can talk in that little room, there, without anyone overhearing what we have to say. Besides, we can show a light without catching the eye of that sharp fiend, Little Billy."

"That little nuisance, eh?" muttered the other, and, following Jim across the hall, he closed the door as soon as both were in the room. Then he switched on a pocket electric torch and laid it on the table between them. The shaft of light blared out against the wall at the end of the room in a crisply defined circle, but it illumined the faces of the two men only dimly. It showed Charlie wearing the bushy red hair that curled under the brim of his sombrero—the red hair that was the distinctive mark, along with the white horse in the trees below—of The Red Devil, that most elusive, most unmerciful outlaw.

He seemed particularly contented with himself now; taking a chair without too much caution, he leaned back in it.

"Well, my friend," he said, "what do you think of the way I've played your rôle? Did you ever make as much money in six weeks as I've made?"

"I don't know how much money you've

made," said Jim, "but I'll tell you this . . . you've acted like a mad dog."

"Look out. You can't talk like that to me."

There was a sudden explosion in Jim. It did not show in a loud voice or a violent gesture or stamp of his foot, but it could be felt as distinctly as though he had done all of these things. He leaned across the table, and in the moment of hush the sound of his hard breathing was audible. Charlie shrank from him. Even in his rôle of The Red Devil, he dared not confront the passion of the man across the table, leaning there veiled in the semidarkness.

"You hound," said Jim at last. "In all my life I've never taken a penny from a gent that hadn't first got that penny by crooked work of some sort. In all the years that I've rode the mountains, I've never killed a man. And you . . . you've played the game for money and death the minute you got on Meg. You've run through the mountains like a mad dog. I said it before. I say it again. Talk up to me, Charlie Mark. Talk up to me. Put a hand on your gun. Cuss me. I'm waiting."

Charlie Mark was not a coward. But he did not choose to answer at that particular instant. He would as soon have twitched a tiger's beard at that moment as to have raised voice or hand against Jim Curry.

"I ought to take that mask. I ought to take

Meg," said Jim. "I ought to get out of this honest home and stay out. I ought to keep you from going back to work as The Red Devil, as they call it. But you've run amuck. You've tasted killing. And you can't be kept at home now. You've gone bad once, and you're the kind that'll stay bad. I know. I've done wrong in ever changing parts with you. I never should've let you take my horse and my mask. But how could I tell then what was inside of you?"

"What made you give the mask to anybody?" queried Charlie Mark, recovering his breath and at last a part of his courage when he saw that Jim Curry did not intend to translate his anger into gun play. "Why didn't you just burn the mask?"

"And what would I do with Meg?"

"Burn her . . . dig a grave for her and shoot her on the edge of it. You could have done that."

There was a strangling sound in the throat of Jim. "You're a devil," he muttered at last. "A plain devil. But I tell you this, Charlie Mark, if ever you do that for Meg, make sure that I'm dead first. Otherwise I'd be on your trail *pronto*." He paused, and then continued with a sudden softening: "How is Meg?"

"Clean as a whip and fit as a fiddle. She's outside. Want to see her?"

"I don't dare. I couldn't keep off her back once I saw her, and, once on her back, I'd be out raising the old deviltry again, I guess."

"You'll be back at it, anyway, one of these days," said Charlie Mark.

"Will I? Well, I dunno, Charlie. I got to confess that it's a temptation that I never get far away from. If it wasn't for this kid, Little Billy, and . . . ."

"And Ruth, I suppose?" Charlie's voice held a sneer.

"Well? You hate her, I guess, because she hates you. But I'll tell you the truth . . . it's for her and Little Billy that I'm keeping straight."

"Wait till your leg's well. You'll be off like a rocket."

"I hope not. And what about you, Charlie? Don't you ever wish that you could get back here?"

"Sure. So I came down and looked the old place over. And now I'm through with it."

"And you're not particular keen to see Henry Mark, the gent that adopted you?"

"Why should I see him? He's nothing in my young life now, my friend. He took me into his family without asking my permission. Well, I'm stepping out again without asking his. What could be fairer than that?"

Jim could not speak. He had met heartless men in his own wild career as an outlaw, the originator of that semi-fabulous character, The Red Devil, but he had never yet met with such utter callousness of mind.

"You're going back now?" he asked at length.

"I'm going back."

"Then go out on the far side of the house and whistle for Meg . . . the same whistle that I taught you. Call her over. You'd better not come close to Little Billy. He's out there, under the trees, near to Meg."

"I'm going . . . I'm going," said the other irritably. "Don't rush me. I looked about my room tonight, and I see that it's where you're sleeping."

"They've given me a bed there."

"And books, and everything like that. I see Ruth's hand in it."

"She's been kind to me."

Charlie chuckled. "Do me good," he said, "if she were to grow fond of The Red Devil. Well, Jim, good bye. Anything you want? Anything you need?"

"Only one thing. I want you to try to get shut of that red mask and lay your plans for jumping the country, Charlie."

"And come back here? *Bah!* Another month of this sort of work, and I'll have a fortune to retire on. Besides, I don't want to retire. You couldn't hire me to give up my work for a thousand dollars a day. There's too much fun in it. So long!"

He slipped through the door and ran, careless of the noise he made, down the back stairs up which Jim Curry had mounted. A few moments later Jim heard a whistle. Then he saw, from the window, a streak of pale gray as Meg raced to her new master. The shouting of Bill was high and shrill in the distance as The Red Devil darted away into the dusk of the night.

Jim leaned out the window to watch, and, so leaning, his left hand slipped and a sharp, projecting nail slashed him across the wrist. He covered the wounded place with an exclamation, and still he watched the disappearing fugitive. And he could scarcely help shouting encouragement after gallant Meg.

In the meantime, the house was waking to noisy life. But Jim sank in his chair. Let them ride their heads off in pursuit, if they wished. He knew too much about Meg and her rider to wish to capture them.

IV

The shouting of Little Billy roused the household of Henry Mark, but Charlie Mark, vanishing into the moon haze on Meg, laughed back at the diminishing sounds of tumult. What did the excitement or the wrath of man mean so long as he had the matchless speed of Meg under him? He could ride in circles around the fastest horses in the corrals of Mark, he knew. Therefore he made no particular effort to put distance between him and the house.

132

As a matter of fact, he knew that there was little need of hurry. Men were so accustomed to consider the speed of Meg as invincible that they rarely, if ever, made a determined attempt to overtake her. To that, in the first place, he had owed the immunity that he enjoyed when he was committing his first crimes and depredations in the new rôle of The Red Devil. They had resisted him in only a half-hearted manner, and they had pursued him with little energy. Why strike back at The Red Devil when to do so was simply to call down further disaster on one's head? They were beginning to treat him as savages treat a sinister deity, to be feared but not to be thwarted for dread of greater vengeance.

These facts were running lazily through the mind of Charlie Mark as the young fellow swept down the valley on Meg, casting about in his mind for some manner in which he might amuse himself. The house of his adopted father was out of sight, and therefore out of mind. He cared not a snap of his fingers for what might come behind him in the shape of pursuit. But he must have excitement to occupy him before morning.

It had grown to be a necessity, just as alcohol is necessary to the drunkard and drugs to the drug addict; within the compass of every two or three days Charlie Mark had to tempt fortune in some manner. Otherwise, he felt that his precious time was wasted. The world was getting out of touch with The Red Devil, and that would never do.

What attracted him this night was the glimmer of the lights of the town just before him, a low, broken line of lights among the trees just down the valley from the house of his adopted father. And toward it, accordingly, Charlie Mark directed Meg. What he would do when he got inside the town, he had not the slightest idea, but something, he was sure, would come to his mind. Something always did.

In this careless mood, then, he swung the mare to the left, made a brief detour, and then left Meg standing among the trees. He advanced from this point on foot, secure from observation in the dimness of the light of the young moon, and tingling to his fingertips with expectation.

As he walked, he made up his mind that something new must be tried. He had never yet shown himself as The Red Devil, secured from recognition only by the mask. Better still, he had never yet heard of The Red Devil venturing among the habitations of man with nothing over his face to hide his identity. Charlie Mark tucked the handkerchief back under the edge of his hat. Making a second detour, he entered fairly upon the head of the street and walked down through the town. There was nothing now to disguise him save the darkness, which there was sufficient moonlight to thin treacherously. Besides, now and again he had to walk through a bright shaft of lamplight.

He would not be recognized as The Red Devil, to be sure, but he was among men every one of whom knew him as the adopted son of Henry Mark. They knew his voice and all his ways— strange indeed that they did not pay attention to him. However, as a matter of fact, not an eye glanced after him even in suspicion. A group of young men shouldered him out of their way, and he submitted simply because he was thinking, with a grin, of how terrible would be their fear if they so much as dreamed that he was The Red Devil. He paused at another corner to listen to the sound of a piano and a girl's voice singing. How marvelously clear the lightest sound became in the quiet atmosphere of the town. He could pick up the noise of a dozen different voices at various angles as he stood there. In the pause of a song there was the *clatter* of pans from a kitchen nearby, and then the crying of a child far off, and a deep man's voice, thunderously low, speaking from a front porch.

Charlie Mark allowed those sounds to sink slowly into his mind. They created there a strange calm, which he had almost forgotten could exist in the world. But presently he was walking on again. Calm was not what he wanted. He could find plenty of that among the mountains, to be sure, but here in town he wanted other things. Grown men were around him, and grown men meant a chance for action.

To the left, for instance, he could find action in plenty, for that was the sheriff's house. Suddenly Charlie halted. In all the tales he had heard, there was no description of a sheriff being held up in his own house in his own town. The heart of Charlie Mark leaped. Perhaps he could make history once more. At least he would try.

He walked down the street a short distance, turned to his left, cut in behind the long row of back yards with their wood sheds and horse sheds, and so came to the ampler barn of the sheriff. How well he remembered it, even out of his childhood, and how greatly he had admired in those days the gilded weathercock on the top of the barn.

Those days were long since past. Charlie Mark turned in toward the back of the sheriff's house, slipped up the stairs to the porch, and listened. He heard a faint murmur of voices, but he could not distinguish the words. Two men were talking. And two men might be rather difficult to handle.

He opened the door. At once the closer, warmer atmosphere of the house rolled out about him, and there was a faint scent of sweets. There had been much baking of spiced cake in the house this day, perhaps.

Then he stepped in, closing the door behind him with the instinctive skill of the robber and worker by night. Now he could make out the voices far more distinctly. They were in the parlor, and one of them was the sheriff himself. No, they were not in the parlor, but in the little library just behind the parlor. The door to the library was open, which allowed the voices to swell down the hall to him. But the parlor itself held different company.

He could make out the jangle of three or four women's voices, always at least two of them in action, and the sounds crossing and jarring and harmonizing. He shivered. He remembered the horror of that jargon when he had been dragged along by his mother in his boyhood when she went calling. It had been a terrific effort to keep from being lulled to sleep, aside from the prickling, sweating agony of having all eyes and voices focus on him as his mother commented on his "points". Something of the old emotion came back to Charlie Mark, and then he chuckled. What a rare joke it would be to hold-up the sheriff in one room while his wife continued to talk on in the next room.

Still smiling at this idea, Charlie continued his advance down the hall until a sudden gust of wind struck his back. Instantly he side-stepped behind a curtain and draped its folds about him, knowing that his boots would be showing beneath, but praying that they might not be discovered, if, as he surmised, the draft meant the opening of a door and the entrance of someone into the hall.

He was right, for now he heard the *swishing* of skirts—at least it was only a woman, the Lord be praised—and then a light gleamed faintly through the fabric of the curtain, shone close at hand, and went on. If she had seen the boots below the curtain, she had made no sign, either by crying out or quickening or retarding her pace. And such self-control was incredible. Another door opened and closed. The light went out. The woman obviously had gone into the parlor, perhaps carrying refreshments.

Charlie Mark, breathing more easily, stepped out from his wretched place of concealment into the hall and again approached the door of the library.

"But what," the voice of the sheriff was saying distinctly, "was behind your wanting to see me tonight, eh?"

"More facts about the gent that calls himself Jim and stays out to the Mark place."

"*Bah!* You're crazy on that subject, Lang."

Charlie Mark started. Was this the Lang who had been in the stage with him when Jim Curry committed his last crime in the rôle and disguise of The Red Devil and held up the coach? Venturing to the corner of the door, he peered within and saw that it was indeed Lang, now sitting bolt upright, flushed with interest, and facing a frowning, dubious host in the sheriff.

"Am I crazy?" said Lang. "I tell you, Sheriff, I've met a man that's plumb sure that this fellow is a gent that used to be called by name of Jim Curry down south. I forget the name of the town it happened in. Anyway, this Curry . . . which is the last name of Jim, according to the stranger . . . left town *pronto* and in a big hurry, because his dad had been killed for murder and he was wanted for stealing horses the same day."

"By the Lord!" exclaimed the sheriff. He added: "But don't you see, Lang, that he can't be The Red Devil? Why, The Red Devil must be middle-aged from the list of the things he's done."

"I've traced him back," said Lang soberly. "He ain't been working more'n six years. And it was just six years ago that Jim Curry was run out of his home town for the reasons I been telling you. I tell you, Sheriff, it's plumb certain that he's the man . . . and the gent that's been running around and raising the devil is simply a gent that's borrowed his horse. It's his partner. That would explain how The Red Devil was always able to make such long jumps between jobs. Work here one day, stick up somebody else eighty miles away tomorrow, and work seventy miles farther on the day after that."

"Hmm," said the sheriff. "I got to admit that this is worth looking into. It don't sound possible, but queer things will happen now and then,

especially when you're hunting somebody like The Red Devil."

"You're right," said a voice from the door.

They turned of one accord. In the doorway stood the familiar figure of The Red Devil. The handkerchief clothed his face save for the eye-holes. The red, bushy hair thrust out beneath his hat. In his hand was a long, black revolver held with convincing steadiness and directed toward them.

V

The amazement of valiant Sheriff Nance at this sight was so great as to be well nigh painful. The worthy man of the law gaped twice like a fish newly taken out of water. Then a motion of the muzzle of Charlie Mark's revolver jerked him out of the water as though an invisible line were indeed attached to him. He rose from his chair and with a gesture persuaded Lang to uncoil his lengthy form and imitate the good example. And when the arms of Lang were extended to the full above his head, his hands nearly touched the ceiling. He looked like one about to strike a smaller opponent into the earth.

"Now," said Charlie Mark, "take the key out of your right-hand vest pocket and throw it down on the carpet near the safe."

140

The sheriff paled. He was an old-fashioned man, so much so that he followed the maxim, "a bird in the hand is worth two in the bush," to a ridiculous extreme, and when he made a profit in money, he deposited it in greenbacks in the capacious drawers of his safe. And being the owner of a large and prosperous ranch, his profits were very great indeed. Of old Charlie knew that the key to that safe was invariably carried in the aforementioned pocket. Had he not in person seen the sheriff produce it more than once and use it to unlock the heavy door with its many layers of strong steel?

A desperate gleam in the eye of the sheriff was correctly interpreted by the robber.

"If you throw that key through the window, Sheriff," he said quietly, "I'll send a chunk of lead to visit your insides. Understand? Do what I tell you. Keep your other hand up while you do it. Don't talk loud."

The sheriff hesitated through another instant, but the steadiness of the revolver in the hand of the outlaw, and withal a certain carelessness with which the fellow managed it, were marvelously convincing. Nance jerked the key from the designated pocket with thumb and forefinger and tossed it onto the carpet just in front of the safe. He did it with a faint accompanying groan that brought a sympathetic murmur from The Red Devil himself.

In the interval of silence the drone of women's voices from the adjoining room buzzed strongly through the folding doors that were all that separated them from the scene of the outrage. And there was something so pleasantly ludicrous to Charlie Mark in the incongruity of the scene that he chuckled softly to himself. He measured Lang with a glance. Plainly the tall man would be the less formidable of the two—the one who could be better trusted to use his hands.

"Go over there and unlock that safe," he commanded.

Lang obeyed meekly, lowering his arms as though the elbow joints were rusted. He knelt by the door, inserted the grating key, and then turned it. The heavy door swung lazily open and revealed a neat row of mahogany shelves, one fitted closely above the other, with a row of small drawers below the shelves. Here the documents and here the cash of the sheriff's saving had been accumulated and stored for many a year.

Charlie Mark could hear the irregular, panting breath of the man of the law, and for the least moment he was on the verge of abandoning his scheme in sheer pity for Nance. But pity was not familiar to Charlie Mark. It never had been in the past, and assuredly this was not an auspicious hour for commencing. He hardened himself with a slight effort and favored Nance with a scowl. In the old days Nance had often been kind to him. But he must not allow these small considerations to interfere. He had work before him—work that must be performed. Moreover, he was perpetrating a jest over which the entire range of the mountain desert would be laughing before the next day was ended.

He backed Lang against the wall in turn, knelt, and, fumbling with his left hand, dragged out drawers and the contents of shelves. A great mass of papers of all kinds tumbled out, rustling on the floor. The stacks of greenbacks were a liberal portion of the litter. They might have been much greater had not the sheriff made a large purchase of property only a few days before. But as it was, Charlie Mark's heart leaped as he crammed the loot into his coat pockets. He had come for a rare jest; he had found, in addition, a fortune awaiting him. How much he picked up, he could not, of course, guess, but he shrewdly estimated by the haggard look of the sheriff that he was taking at least a large part of the hoardings of a life of industry and prosperity.

When he rose, his coat pockets were swelled out on either side. He was carrying with him enough to retire on. He could leave the mountains if he wished, and go East, and appear there with hands washed clean of all connection with the murders and robberies that he had committed in the far West.

With this in mind he slipped back to the door and hesitated there with murder in his heart. No matter how he bound these two, the least noise after his departure would bring to their assistance the women of the next room, and then they would be after him. But suppose he were to touch the trigger twice from the doorway. He would send to death those two formidable fighters, and free his trail from immediate pursuit. So he hesitated in the doorway with his grip tightening and loosening around the butt of the gun. And it seemed from the pallor of the two who were backed against the wall with their hands high above their heads that they read in the burning eyes, which they saw through the holes in the handkerchief, the purpose that was forming in the brain of The Red Devil. They shrank back, flattening themselves against the wall as though they half hoped that a secret door might unfold behind them and give them a chance for flight. Then the balance turned in the cruel mind of Charlie Mark. Fierce though his instincts were, he could not kill two helpless men.

He leaped to one side and raced down the hall. The screen door was kicked open before him, and he plunged into the welcome darkness of the night. At the same instant a window was dragged screamingly open, and through the aperture the sheriff and Lang blazed forth a hail of shots after the fugitive. One of them clipped the skin and the surface flesh of his left wrist as he swung it back in the midst of a stride. That sting gave him greater speed to gain the trees; he urged Meg on as the riot of noise issued from the house and was taken up on either hand, that ringing call— "The Red Devil!"—serving to bring men instantly out of their homes armed and ready to shoot to kill.

It was miraculous, the speed with which they got into the saddle, these townsmen. Confident that once he reached the back of Meg he was as safe as though he had been whisked into the clouds, Charlie Mark drew the mare down to a rocking canter and looked back with a careless smile at the line of trees that masked the lights of the village. It would be minutes before horsemen issued from it. Then would come a headlong dash of three or four miles, barely enough to make Meg extend herself and start her circulation. After that they would give up as they had given up so many times before.

But he was in this case sadly mistaken. Hardly had he cleared the trees when man after man shot out of the darkness, riding low on their horses and driving them to the full of their speed. It was almost as though they had been lying in wait.

In that case they would have such riding tonight as they had never enjoyed before. He called on Meg, and she answered with a swinging gallop deceptively slow and easy to watch, but in reality far swifter than the labored and pounding gallop of the cow ponies behind her.

Charlie Mark looked back again. There were half a dozen men shouting and racing in the lead. Behind them others and still others were issuing from the trees. Guns began to spurt red tongues of fire here and there. A bullet *hummed* close to his head. Moreover, his left wrist was stinging. Enraged, he whirled in the saddle with gun poised. Once, twice, and again he fired, and two horsemen plunged to the earth. He had aimed for the horses rather than the men, and he grunted savage satisfaction as he saw them drop. They were not dead, perhaps, but they were badly wounded. And dead or wounded made no difference to Charlie Mark. He wanted liberty and a chance to bandage that wounded wrist. *Ah*, now he would have what he wanted, for the crowd began to fall back; Meg began to draw away with her matchless gait.

It was not all the speed of Meg, however. Sheriff Nance, riding in the forefront of the pursuit, had seen his two neighbors go down beside him, and had heard the *hum* of a bullet pass the head of his own horse. He drew his companions back with a shout and a wave of the hand. Especially he called Lang to him.

"Boys," he said, "I want you to keep back at a steady pace. I'll show you the way. Lang, you turn around and go back to town as fast as your hoss will take you. Get to a telephone, and wire ahead to Elmira Junction. The Red Devil is riding like a fool or a crazy man. He's going straight up to the narrows, and, if Elmira turns out, they'll bag him sure."

Lang was comparatively new to the region, but he had seen a map of the district. He gathered at once the simple plan of the sheriff, which was so clear to the others, also, that it drew a yell of exultation from them. The valley in which the town lay was shaped like a spoon, and Charlie Mark, heedless of everything except a desire to put distance between him and the pursuit, was driving straight into the handle of the spoon. In that handle lay the village of Elmira. By telephoning ahead, it should be easy to draw out the men of the town into a cordon extending clear across the floor of the valley. On either side were hills with precipitous slopes. They could be scaled, but they could hardly be negotiated with a horse. And if The Red Devil wished to turn aside from the converging lines of his enemies, he would have to leave Meg behind him, which was something that not one of the pursuers believed that the outlaw would do. Villainous he had shown himself on countless occasions, but there was a profoundly based belief through the mountains that The Red Devil loved his horse as though it were a human being and would not desert it under any consideration. Into how tight a hole might that love for the horse drag him?

At any rate, Lang jerked his horse around and spurred back toward town as though he were racing to reach the gates of his salvation.

VI

In the meantime, Meg swung along with tireless ease and speed. She had traveled a great distance that day, and she had behind her the challenge of fresh horses. To be sure, she could distance them in a sprint, but, on the other hand, they could hang in the rear upon her trail as tireless as wolves. They would never give up the work, those dauntless little cow ponies behind her. And now as Charlie Mark, after attaining what he considered a safe lead, stopped to tie up his injured wrist, he was interrupted before the completion of that leisurely job by the dull roar of hoof beats behind him as they ground over a wide bed of gravel.

He finished tying the knot, and then raised his handsome head and looked back over his shoulder with something between a sneer and a snarl. That wolfish glance to the rear satisfied him that the pursuers had not yet given up the task of hounding him. And he shook his head in amazement. They were not wont to plunge away blindly through the night behind him. As a rule there was just that opening spurt to overtake him and then, for two or three days, an aimless wandering here and there through the mountains in vague hope of crossing his path. Tonight, however, different tactics were being followed. They clung behind him as though the nose of a hound were showing them the way.

When he had made up his mind that they were there, however, he simply shrugged his shoulders and loosened the rein. White Meg would do the rest.

She showed a nice turn of speed for the next couple of miles, and, although he could tell by the slight labor of her gallop that she was far from fresh, yet she left the cow ponies behind her like the wind. At the end of that burst he slowed her again.

They had entered the narrow part of the valley. The hills arose on either hand, well nigh as steep as the surfaces of a cliff. And as he drew the mare down to a more reasonable pace, he could hear in the distance behind him the faint sound of the posse still galloping, the noise traveling dimly to the hills and being reëchoed still more lightly from them.

This was puzzling in the extreme. Did the fools think that they could run down Meg? He chuckled at the mere suggestion of such an idea and sent her on briskly once more.

He diverged well to the right to avoid the out-skirts of the town of Elmira Junction, so called because here the two main roads of the valley joined. On swept Meg, never faltering, but tossing her fine head a little now and then as though inquiring the reason for this extraordinary demand. Since morning, when she left the cave, she had had little rest that day. The old master would never have made such a call upon her strength. But then, there were many differences between the old master and the new, and this was only a small sign of them.

They were in the very center of the narrows, as that cañon was called throughout the neighbor-ing district, when, running up a slight slope toward a cresting line of shrubs that topped it, he was received with a sudden explosion of a rifle and the shrill, small, wicked singing of a bullet past his head. He halted the mare and whirled her around with a single jerk of his arm. And as she turned, there was a roar of angry voices above him—voices that devoutly cursed the man who had fired too soon and betrayed the existence of the ambush. And through and above that roar of voices came the crash of a volley.

How Charles Mark escaped a dozen bullets in his body by that first smashing volley—how Meg, at least, came off scatheless when by color she was such an ideal mark in the darkness, Charlie Mark could never tell. But the premature shot fired by one man had so upset that ambushed line, waiting as they were for a prearranged signal, that the first fire was wildly delivered. They shot at the mere glimmer of the white mare in the darkness, and the next instant their bullets from the second discharge were plowing through thin air.

The miraculous disappearance of horse and rider caused the whole line of the watchers, who had ridden out of Elmira Junction in response to the frantic appeals of Lang, to leave their ambush and come at the run, shouting and brandishing their rifles above their heads, for they naturally took it for granted that horse and rider had gone to earth, shot through and through, and so disappeared in a small hollow.

It was no small hollow, however, into which The Red Devil and his horse had dropped. Just to the left as he whirled the mare about, Charlie Mark saw a sharply cut depression hollowed out by action of rainwater during some torrential downpour. Into that little gulley he sent catfooted Meg with one touch of his heels. Out of sight she dropped into the pit of darkness, staggered in the uneven footing, and then sped like the wind down the valley in the same direction from which she had come.

When Charlie Mark spurred the mare out of the shelving gully a hundred yards farther down, the pursuit was already thrown into the comparative distance. Panting from their run as they saw the dim figure twinkle again in front of them, they halted, pitched rifles to their shoulders, and blazed away at random. Charlie Mark, with only the occasional waspish *hum* of a bullet to annoy him, reined Meg into a thicket and rode on, breathing more freely. On the whole it had been his closest call so far.

His feeling of exultation, however, lasted only a few moments, for coming up the valley he heard a wide-spreading rushing of hoofs sounding like the approach of a distant wave of hail beating over the forest. He knew, of course, that it was the original group of manhunters now pressing steadily after their prey.

And a sudden sense of doom struck Charlie Mark for the first time, whipped the color out of his head, and covered his forehead with cold perspiration. He had started with a sneer of contempt for the men behind him. That sneer he had repeated time and again as the sound of their galloping horses reached him, but every time he considered himself safe from them, he heard that dull pounding once more. Was it fated that after all he was to meet his end from those men who had ridden out to avenge the insult and the loss of the sheriff?

He twitched Meg to the left and made for the dark-faced hill in that direction, a considerable stretch, before he remembered that the slopes of those hills were practically impossible for horses to climb. Then, with a savage curse directed at his own stupidity, he jerked Meg about and drove her down the valley again.

Guns were now exploding behind him and before—not shots directed at him, he could very well guess, but shots meant as signals from the rear party to the party in front. It began to be obvious. In some manner they had communicated with Elmira Junction, and they had spread a net into which he ran—like a fool! Only then he remembered the telephone and its possibilities—that newly strung telephone across the wide stretch of country. He raised his fist and shook it against the spirit of science that had so worked against him this night of nights.

He drew rein. Speed was not the thing he needed now. But when he tried to think, the heaving sides of Meg disturbed him. She was far spent. She had not many more fast miles in her that night, no matter how gallant her heart. And now the men of Elmira Junction were crashing in behind him on fresh horses, yelling and whooping like Indians in their certainty that they were about to bag game. And such game.

Again Charlie Mark clenched his fist and bared his teeth like a cornered wolf. Suppose he were to leave Meg and take to the hills on foot? No, they would find the horse at once, and, while some of them combed the immediate

153

vicinity of the trees, others would swarm up over the hills. And without a horse, ignorant of the exact nature of the ground, he would be found, no matter how fast he climbed.

Behind and in front, now, the shouts increased. There was no longer a firing of guns. They were calling to one another in long, wailing voices, pitched to cut through the distance. They were joining hands to hem him in—curse them! In the fullness of his hatred it did not occur to him that he had done things to rouse such consuming fury against him. It only seemed brutal waste of energy for so many men to be hounding one. He listened sharply. The original band, on tired horses, pressed ahead slowly, apparently ready to receive a surprise attack from the outlaw, shouting far less often than the men from Elmira, who were riding in with yells of triumph that rushed with increasing speed on the ear of the robber.

There was nothing else for it. At least he would die like a man, instead of like a rat. He turned Meg, picked what seemed to be a rift between two yelling groups of the riders from Elmira, and jogged the mare ahead. Presently she reached the edge of the trees, and across the clearing beyond swept the avengers, a cloud on either side—a cloud of half a dozen men ready to shoot to kill.

Charlie Mark flattened himself along the neck of Meg. He clung to her, whispering a frantic appeal for speed in her quivering ear. Then he gave her the spurs.

She answered it like a two-year-old newly turned from pasture into corral and raging against confinement. She leaped away with as much life as an uncoiling watch spring, plunged past the skirting trees, and darted into the open.

By sheer good luck the ground over which she raced was soft woodland mold. It was wretched ground for speed, but it gave a priceless advantage to make up for such a handicap. It enabled Meg to rush out from the trees in utter silence. And she was halfway across the clearing, soundless as a running cloud shadow, before a shrill yell went up from the men of Elmira, and they swung their horses about, facing in.

In that confused maneuver of turning they lost a few precious seconds, but what else could they do? The outlaw was between two parties, and a shot aimed at him would be more than likely to miss and take effect on one of the townsmen on the opposite side. They could only turn and wait for a chance to shoot from behind.

That chance came at once. The two parties revolved and faced in the opposite direction, and then, as they raised their guns, they saw Meg slip like a phantom among the trees. They fired, but the only result was the crashing of the bullets among the branches. Then they pressed in to make another trial of speed with Meg.

She was nearly done, poor Meg, but answered that new challenge with a courage and heart worthy of another cause. Straightaway she burst into a gallop well nigh as light and as sweeping as the step with which she had darted down among the boulders of the hillside early that same day. It was a delusive lightness, to be sure, supplied by strength of spirit rather than strength of muscle, but the first three miles were dizzy miles to follow, and sent the sweat pouring and dripping down the shoulders of the horses from Elmira.

Still they pressed on. Sheriff Nance, mounted freshly by courtesy of an Elmira citizen, continued to lead, heartening his men at every step. They circled around from the end of the spoon-handle of the narrow valley and up through the rougher and higher mountains again. Speed of foot was the least requirement for progress now. There was needed to a far greater degree the leathery endurance and the climbing ability of a mountain sheep. Here the horses of the cowpunchers excelled. Even when fresh, Meg would not have had a great advantage over them. Half exhausted as she was, they now gained upon her at a deadly rate.

Still The Red Devil pressed on in what seemed to the sheriff and his companions an insane direction. He was not heading for a stretch of level land where he might use the speed of Meg to vital advantage again. Instead, he was driving her remorselessly into the rough going, and up steeper and steeper grades.

"We'll get him now, lads!" called one of the men as they saw the figure of The Red Devil sketched against the moon haze in the sky at the top of a tall cliff. "We'll get him now! He can't ride Meg down through thin air, I reckon!"

So, indeed, he could not, and that impossibility was not his intention.

"It's the end of him!" cried the sheriff in great excitement. "He's cornered, and he ain't going to let his hoss live after him. He's going to jump Meg over the cliff and die with her. Look at him!"

Charlie Mark had turned in the saddle and was shaking his fist at the small blots that were the signs of men swarming in pursuit of him across the ground below. Then he swung out of the stirrups and landed lightly on the ground beside Meg and was seen to step to the edge of the precipice.

For the first time his purpose became clear to the sheriff, and with a yell he warned his companions. "Ride, boys, ride! He's going to leave Meg! Who'd ever believe that? He's going to leave Meg behind him, after all the times she's saved him. Feed the hosses the spur!"

He set the example, rushing his horse at the grade, while the form of Charlie Mark was lost to view. They stormed up to the height, and there they found Meg standing with her head down and her legs spread and braced, so great was her exhaustion. When they swept around her, she merely tossed up her head, but she made no move to escape them.

When they leaned over the cliff, however, they received a different greeting. It was the ringing explosion of a rifle far down the precipice, which drove them quickly back. Their hands were tied so far as The Red Devil was concerned. They had taken his horse, but at that price he had escaped them. To climb down the cliff after him, in face of his rifle fire, was impossible. To make the long detour on either side would require too much time. He had simply slipped through their fingers. Nevertheless, they had a feeling of triumph that the sheriff very aptly phrased.

"He's been beat for the first time," he said. "We have chased him a pile of times before, but we never so much as touched a hair of him. Now we have his horse. And what's more, we've nicked The Red Devil himself enough to see red. Look there!"

Even by moonlight they could see it. Crimson from the wounded left wrist of Charlie Mark had stained the horn of the saddle, the shoulder of Meg, and her flank.

"We've got his horse," continued the sheriff grimly, "and he's got away with the work of my life in money. Well . . . I guess it's a fair exchange."

VII

From the room in the house of Henry Mark, Jim
Curry had watched the glimmering shape of Meg
begin her flight. Then he had waited while the
shrill voice of Little Billy alarmed the house and
started the cowpunchers from the bunkhouse
into the quiet air of the night. In a few seconds
more he was able to watch the whole cavalcade
thundering off into the night and sweeping up
toward the broad end of the valley. But he
shrugged his shoulders, quite indifferent to the
fate of the riders.

Whatever betided, they would not capture the
rider of Meg. He had bestrode her too often to
dream that the best horses on the Mark place
could so much as force her into a sweat on a hot
day. Besides, they were probably taking the
wrong direction. They rode toward the broad end
of the valley, because they took it for granted
that the robber would not dare ride toward the
town. But would not this be the reason Charlie
Mark would prefer that direction for his flight?
He himself, had he been playing his old rôle,
would not have fled at all, but, having bolted
toward the trees, he would have reined Meg to
one side or the other, waited for the manhunters
to crash by him, and then he might have cantered

a little distance in their rear to watch the pro-
ceedings.

Charlie Mark no doubt lacked the coolness to
do such a thing, but he might very well have
sense enough to take the least-suspected road
and ride toward the town. So in a mood of perfect indifference Jim Curry watched the riders
stream off into the night, among them Little
Billy himself—Little Billy riding valorously to
take his place in the manhunt. Jim Curry grinned
at the thought, but his smile did not wear well.
He was sober again in a moment.

After all, they were riding in pursuit of a fiend
in human shape who he, Jim Curry, had raised
and given identity. Driven out from among his
fellow men by a combination of hard luck and
youthful hot-headedness years ago, he himself
had created the rôle that Charlie Mark was now
playing to the tune of murder and outrage. And
he felt as though he had made a new Franken-
stein and turned it loose on a suffering world.

In that gloomy mood he leaned at the window
and pondered. He had done many a bad thing,
but never had he done so wicked a deed as when
he allowed Charlie Mark to take his place, accept
the disguise and the horse of The Red Devil, and
turn the ruthless fellow loose on the mountain
desert.

After a time, he roused himself and went
slowly down the back stairs. Walking slowly,

noiselessly, as he always walked, he passed through the lower floor of the house and came to the parlor, where the light announced the presence of Ruth Mark. He parted the stiff folds of the curtain and looked inside.

She sat by the window on the far side of the room, her profile, cut clear as a chisel cuts white marble, against that background of darkness, her hands fell idly into her lap. She was looking at the ceiling and beyond the ceiling into gloomy thoughts of her own.

He knew by the true voice of instinct that, if he entered, she would start up with a smile. But he did not enter. He had no right, he told himself bitterly, to make her smile in that manner. Later on some of the truth about his past would begin to leak out, in spite of himself, and then she would loathe him. It was inevitable. He was enjoying in this home the rest of a traveler who reaches an oasis, but who knows that in a short space he must go on again and face the blinding heat and the storms of the desert. Staring at her, Jim Curry knew that she was all to him that the green tops of the palms are to the Bedouin when he sights them far away, with a pale-blue sky behind and a white-hot desert in front. But he let the stiff curtain fold fall slowly, softly together and drew back with the same noiseless footfall into the hall.

However noiseless his footfall, however, it

seemed that the stir of the curtain had attracted her attention. Presently there was a rush of tapping slipper heels, the curtains were flung wide apart, and framed in the triangle of drapery was Ruth Mark, peering eagerly into the darkness before her. The hall lamp had been turned down too low; it was a glowing spot in the solid dark rather than a point of illumination.

"Jim," called the girl softly. "Jim, was that you?" She waited. Her head was canted.

He could see her smile of expectancy, and he wanted with all his heart to go toward her, but he dared not trust himself. It was too easy to talk to her. It would be too easy to say too much. He waited until, with a faint exclamation of disappointment, she let the curtain fall together again and was gone.

Then he turned and continued his retreat, wondering. How quick her ear was. Out of profoundest meditation, how swiftly she had run toward him. If he should go back to her now, ask her why she had called, sit near her, begin to tell her all those things that were swelling and stirring in his heart—how would she answer him? He could not doubt what that answer would be. And suppose that, after he had roused and wakened her heart toward him, he were then to tell her the truth about his past and all of his doings as The Red Devil? After all, they were not so very black. He had robbed, but he had never robbed the poor. He had shot men down, but he had never killed. And although they loaded his reputation with a hundred grim murders, attributing to the mysterious rider of the white horse all the unexplainable crimes in the mountains, he could persuade her that force of circumstance had compelled him to what he had done, and that it had never driven him to take life or oppress the weak.

Yes, he could make her believe all of this, and no doubt he could, in the impulse and the great-heartedness of the moment, make her give him a promise that afterward she would keep holy. But would it not be spoiling her life? Would it not be a thing against which she would writhe and revolt later on? Yes, assuredly it would. It would blast her life as well as his own should the truth ever come out. It would drive him into the heart of the mountains again, an outlaw. It would ostracize her as the outlaw's wife.

He closed the rear door of the house softly behind him, full of this thought, and, going to the corral, he caught a horse, saddled, and jogged the nag down the road toward town.

The placid village where he had expected to cant back in a chair whose back rested against the wall of the hotel lobby was, however, in a swirl of excitement. Armed men were mounting and galloping as fast as their horses could carry them toward the far end of the valley. Women and even children were gathered here and there, gossiping. And on every side he heard the name of The Red Devil mixed with breathless exclamations of wonder from the women and deep-throated oaths from the old men.

One of these, wagging his long-bearded head from side to side, he accosted as the veteran was making his way from one cluster to another.

"What's happened?" asked Jim Curry.

"The Red Devil's happened," said the old man. "That's enough. He'll be murdering us in our beds before long. He's held up the sheriff in the sheriff's own house, and he's opened the sheriff's own safe with the sheriff's own key, and dog-gone me if he ain't taken the sheriff's own money and got scat-free away!"

This amazing recital left Jim Curry gasping, and a thrill of excitement went prickling up his spine. In his own most palmy days he had never performed a more hair-raising and successful coup than this. After all, there must be something more in Charlie Mark than the mere instinct for murder. Perhaps such talents, had they been given a chance to develop in the right line, might have made him a man of good influence in society. But the thought had no sooner formed in the brain of Jim Curry than he shook his head. From all he could learn, the nature of Charlie Mark was bad. He had been a sneak and a bully in his childhood. He had been a gambler and a fighter

164

in his manhood. He had begun young, and he was simply continuing the same tactics. That was all there was to it, and it was foolish to take the blame for his present crimes on his own shoulders.

A loud-voiced lamenter now attracted his attention, and he saw two women standing in the center of a group of excited listeners. A hard-faced creature of middle-age made the noise; a withered, kind-eyed old lady was supported on the arm of the virago.

"If it was only part gone, we could stand it," said the declaimer. "But it's all gone . . . all gone. Every cent that ma and me has in the world. I say, speaking personal, that the sheriff and The Red Devil come to an agreement. Why not? The Red Devil comes and scoops up everything. Then he gives back the sheriff's money and part of mine, too. But it ain't me. Not me alone. It's the babies mostly. Why did the sheriff come telling us we'd ought to put everything in his safe where he could keep his eye on it for us? It was only yesterday. . . ."

"Hush, hush," said her old mother. "Come along, honey, and don't be wringin' your hands about spilt milk. We'll live some way. And we'll take care of the babies, Lord bless 'em."

Jim Curry spurred his horse out of hearing of the wail, and with a black face he turned down the street and rode again into the dark valley beyond.

VIII

He rode with an angry determination now, pushing his mount to the limit of its speed, and quite regardless of the occasional twinge of pain in his wounded thigh. That wound, however, was weak rather than still open, and in his present state of mind the pain meant nothing to him. He only allowed the pace to abate when they reached the steep upgrades of the hills.

Once among them, he was at home. He knew every path and pass among the rolling crests. This was his hole-in-the-wall country, in which he had baffled pursuit times beyond number. This was the country of twisting cañons and dry creekbeds, where the blow-sand sifted together and washed out the trace of a hoof print almost as soon as the hoof was withdrawn. Every hill had for Jim Curry a separate story and even a separate character. When he first entered the district he had thought it barren and hard enough. But long acquaintance had made it a kindly place to him.

The darkness did not matter. He knew every stone in every trail, and he pushed the horse remorselessly uphill and down until he came in the vicinity of that well-known hillside where was the entrance to the cave in which he had spent four long years of his life, and where, he had no doubt, Charlie Mark was still dwelling. He would not waste time in looking up another retreat. He would prefer to take it for granted that the original dweller in the cave would never return to disturb his solitude.

In a comparatively short time he reached a steep-sided gorge littered with enormous boulders, each magnified now by shadow in the dimness of the moon shine. Winding among these stones with the precision of old usage, he came to one of the largest of the rocks, swung down from the saddle, threw the reins over the head of his horse, and approached the great stone.

He circled behind it, and, where it leaned against the side of the hill he stooped over, worked a moment at a corner of the rock as though he expected to tear the whole enormous mass from its bed, and then actually succeeded in moving a great slab. This turned inward beneath his pressure and revealed a narrow passage partly natural and partly cleared out by hammer and chisel through the stone.

Down this passage he crept, turned to the right at a narrow elbow bend, and in this manner entered a long, low cave, in the center of which there was the sputtering and uneven light of a small fire whose flames were thrown back and forth and up and down by the action of a random draft. Beside that fire sat Charlie Mark with a rudely improvised table before him, and on the table were little stacks of money that he had arranged in neat piles. And as he contemplated it, he rocked backward and forward, singing softly to himself.

Jim Curry contemplated this figure and his occupation through a moment of silence. Then he stepped boldly into the interior.

"It's me, Charlie!" he called.

At the first sound of his voice there was a remarkable change in the attitude of Charlie Mark. He leaped like an acrobat from his seat, hurled himself sidewise from the fire and into shadow, and whipped out his revolver. But even as he brought it out, he seemed to realize first that the greatest speed in the world could not save him if an enemy had entered the cave and taken him by surprise, also that this was not an enemy at all.

He straightened, therefore, and shoved the revolver back into the holster, and he made himself smile, although his face was still pale as he came toward Jim Curry, who all this time had remained with his nervous right hand resting on his hip, frowningly intent on the movements of Charlie Mark, but disdaining to draw his own gun until the last instant of safety. He approached Charlie in turn, coming into the firelight.

"Hello!" called Charlie Mark. "Seems that you

and I are to see a good deal of each other this evening, eh?" And he extended his hand cordially, although all the time, with a flickering side glance, he was observing his hoard of money spread out so enticingly on the little table, each stack with the pebble placed on top to keep a single bill from blowing away. That extended hand, however, was not taken by Jim Curry. And it dropped sharply back to the side of Mark, where it lingered near the butt of his revolver. He was grinding his teeth with rage, but pretended not to have noticed the slight.

"Sit down and make yourself at home," he said. "You see, I'm just counting over the proceeds of the day's work, Jim. Sit down and have a cup of coffee . . . and something to eat with it, if you're hungry."

"Thanks," said Curry. "I'm not having chow. Not hungry." So saying, he stepped past the other and advanced slowly down the cave with a sauntering step as though he enjoyed looking over the place once more.

The moment he had gone past and his back was turned on Charlie, the latter's fingers closed around his gun butt, but he refrained from drawing the weapon more than halfway out of the holster. A mysterious power, a mysterious fear forced the gun back again. He could not shoot at that courageous back turned so carelessly upon him.

"You've got more horses, I see," said Jim Curry conversationally. Going deep into the shadows, he reached two horses tethered against the wall of rock, their heads turned and their eyes glistening faintly among the shadows. "That bay," he went on, "is a likely stepper, Charlie, and the roan ain't so bad, either. How d'you manage to give 'em both exercise?"

"They get enough," said Charlie Mark, moving back to his store of money that had been stolen from the sheriff.

"*Hmm*," said the other doubtfully. "I don't see how you manage it. All I could do to keep one horse out in the fresh air enough. Horses ain't going to thrive down here underground, Charlie. You can lay to that."

"They thrive enough," said Charlie Mark. He was keen to take up his money and remove that temptation from sight, but he dared not do it. It would be entirely too pointed, he felt. "And what do you think of 'em for speed, Jim?"

Curry was going about them, running his hands over their legs, feeling the bone and the muscle. "Sprinters," he said. "Both of 'em. They got plenty of foot, but how about their staying qualities, Charlie? They don't look like mountain horses to me."

"That roan," exclaimed Charlie Mark indignantly, "stepped a mile within three seconds as fast as the white mare! I sent her over a stretch

170

of good road last week and held a clock on her."

"Sure." Jim Curry nodded. "She done the first mile fast enough, but what about the second mile . . . and what if both of them miles had been done over hills, instead of the level?"

Charlie Mark was silent, biting his lip. It was true that the second mile had shown a great falling off.

"Plenty of horses," said Jim Curry, "could walk away from Meg. I ain't denying that. I never denied it. Take any thoroughbred that's trained for sprinting, and they'll leave Meg behind for the first three or four miles on the level. But races ain't what you want a horse for. You want a horse that can stay all day. You want a horse that can hit a stiff gait and keep to it. Why, in five miles across rough country Meg would kill both them horses, and you'd ought to know it."

Charlie Mark grew dark of brow, but he said nothing; he only murmured unintelligible words.

"You've lost Meg, I see," said Jim Curry in addition. "And I tell you, Charlie, that, without her, you'd a pile better give up the job and get out of the mountains and burn that there red wig." He went on with a growing emotion: "You've lost Meg! Did you ride her to death, Charlie?"

Charlie Mark stepped back into the shadow. There was infinite danger masked behind the gentle tone of Jim Curry. "No," he said hastily. "I didn't ride her to death. What sort of a man do you think I am?"

"Are you lying, Mark?" said Jim, breathing hard.

"I'll swear to you, Jim."

"You don't have to," said Curry. "You're as hard a gent as I ever heard about, but not even you could ride Meg down and leave her. Not even you. What become of her?"

"They had me cornered. I rode her to the top of West Rock and left her there. I climbed down the cliff, and, when they came to the top, I sent a couple of shots up to bother 'em. I think I may have dropped a couple of them, at that."

His eyes glistened at the thought, and Jim Curry shivered.

"You left her, eh? Well, Charlie, you left your own chance of staying on as The Red Devil when you left her. She's gone, and you're done. D'you see that? She's what saved me. She's what saved you all these days. Best thing for you to do is to pack up and go, Mark. Go East and stay East, because once you've run amuck in the West, it ain't a place for a gent like you to stay."

"*Bah!*" answered Charlie Mark, for during the conversation he seemed to have lost much of the awe of his companion that had bothered him after Jim first arrived. "Meg's gone, but I'll go down in a couple of days and steal her back. Watch me, Jim!"

172

"She'll be guarded."

"Never mind the guards. I need her. And what I need, I take. That used to be your way, and now it's my way. They have Meg now. But I'll have her back inside of a day or two."

"I'll make a bet with you on that," said Jim slowly.

"Which way?"

"That you don't get her."

"You will, eh? And why?"

"Because I'm going to get her for myself. Don't you suppose I've been aching for her, Charlie? Why, she and me have been pals." He drew back his head and laughed exultantly. "Don't you see," he explained, "that the only reason I ever let her go was because I had to if I wanted to leave my old life and get back with law-abiding folks? And the only reason I ever let you take my old place was because of Meg . . . there had to be somebody that would care for her . . . and that meant there had to be somebody that would carry on as The Red Devil. But that's ended. You've let her out of your hands. You've let them capture her. And now, when I get her from the sheriff, nobody can ever suspect me of having been The Red Devil."

"But how'll you get her from the sheriff?"

"Can't I buy her? Isn't there enough money there?" And he pointed to the money stacked on the table.

IX

Instantly Charlie Mark became rigid. There was no mistaking the meaning in the glittering eyes of Jim Curry. He meant battle—fierce and sudden battle. And Charlie Mark glared back. He was not afraid. Fear had left him after that first night when as The Red Devil he had taken the first life. Thereafter he had forgotten what fear could be, except once or twice when he was in the presence of Jim Curry. But even Jim Curry became an obstacle not impossible to overcome tonight. He had seemed invincible at first. But now he was only a man. It was a proof that Charlie Mark had advanced very far indeed since the first day when he took up the work of The Red Devil where Jim Curry left it off.

Nevertheless, he wanted time, and for the sake of time he would fence with the other, but he must fence in such a way that he would never be suspected of fearing the conflict.

"That's a rather foolish remark," he said to Curry. "Mighty foolish, Jim, almost any way that you look at it. If you pull a gun, I'll shoot you full of holes. You know that."

Curry shrugged his shoulders. "Listen to me, Charlie," he said. "I ain't up here hankering to do a killing. I never have killed yet, and I don't want to begin now . . . not so much for your sake as for the sake of old man Mark. But if it came to a pinch and I had to make my choice between a dog and you, I'd pick you, Mark. You're a bad one all the way through. I'll tell you what I . . . ."

"Just a minute," said Charlie Mark. "I know that you have learned quite a bit of respectable lingo, Jim. But don't spring it on me. I'm not interested. Wait till you find some blockhead that would believe you."

"I'm going to finish. It won't take long."

"Thanks for that."

"I started up here because I'd heard that half of the money you stole from the sheriff was money that belonged to a widow and her daughter who'd put their savings with the sheriff's for safekeeping . . . ."

"And you wanted to ask me to give back their half?" Charlie Mark laughed at the absurdity of the idea.

"I was going to make you give it back, and let you keep the rest."

"And let me keep it?"

"That's what I mean. Now I've changed my mind."

"You're going to take it all, eh?"

"Exactly."

"You fool, d'you think that I believe for a minute that you'd give back a cent to the old woman?"

"I don't expect you to believe. But it's the truth."

"Besides, Curry, you're a greater fool still for thinking that you can make me do anything. You aren't man enough for the job, my friend. You were in the old days, I admit. But we've changed places in more than name. I'm where you used to be when it comes to fighting, and you're where I was."

"That so?"

"It certainly is. I've practiced every day with rifle and revolver. I took the advice you gave me in the first place, Jim. I followed that advice carefully. I worked for hours every day. I've lived with a revolver until I've got the feel of it. I've labored over the draw and the balance and the whole matter like a musician practicing to become a virtuoso. Understand?"

"That word's a little big for me, son."

"I suppose so. What I mean is that I have worked over the squeeze of the trigger as the violinist works over the technique of bowing. I've learned how to shoot quick and shoot straight. I'm telling you all this, Jim, not because I expect you to believe that I'm a better shot than you are, but just to make you understand that I'm nearly as good, even in your own eyes. Besides, I've shot to kill from the first, and a man who has done that is better than a man who hasn't. You have to admit it."

In fact his discourse had made Jim Curry a trifle thoughtful.

"You talk quite a pile about yourself," said the ex-bandit, smiling at last. "Too much talk and too little action."

"There'll be enough of that when we get started. Don't worry. What I want you to see, Jim, is that I'm not anxious to add you to my list. You've done too much for me for me to pay you back that way now." He consulted his inward sense of danger for an instant and then continued: "I'll tell you what I'll do, Jim. I'll split that pool with you fifty-fifty. You must admit that it's money I got in a way that even you never would have had the nerve to try in your palmiest days. But I'll split that with you and call it square, for the sake of what you did in setting me up in business, as one might put it."

He chuckled contentedly at his own expression. But he saw that Curry was not listening. He was simply studying his companion gravely and in a detached manner, as though there were thin air before him rather than a human being, thin air with a stain of smoke in it.

"It's no good, Charlie," said Jim Curry. "I let you go for the sake of Meg when I seen you at the house this evening. Now I see a way of getting the mare safe without you. And I see it's time that The Red Devil should stop riding the mountains. Understand, Charlie?"

"You mean you're firm that you won't listen to reason?"

"I mean this, Charlie. Sooner or later I think you and me would have to fight. Partly you're right in what you say about you getting better and me getting worse as a fighter. I've found out that a gent can't live quiet and peaceable and away from danger without having his eye get slow and his hand like lead. You see? And here you are up in the mountains living like a wildcat. After a while, if we crossed, we might well be different. You'd be the one with the quick hand and the sure eye, and I'd be the slow one. Maybe that's the way we are right now . . . but I think I have a fighting chance against you, Charlie, and I figure on using it. Are you ready?"

He had spoken so gently and quietly that Charlie Mark was not at all prepared for the sudden revelation of purpose contained in the last words. And then his cunning brain conceived a trick simple enough and the more deadly because of its simplicity. He stretched forth his left hand argumentatively.

"I'm ready," said Charlie. "Still I have one more thing to say, Jim, and that is. . . ."

As he spoke, he flicked the revolver from the holster with his right hand and fired from the hip—once, twice. And for the first time Jim Curry, alias The Red Devil, was beaten to the draw. The trick, no doubt, had much to do with it, but unbelievable speed of finger and wrist also played its part.

Something more than speed is necessary in gun play, however. The revolver of Jim Curry came like a laggard from its leather sheath in comparison with the gun of Charlie Mark, but it exploded just as the second bullet from Mark's gun clipped the hair beside Jim's forehead.

There was no occasion for a fourth shot to be fired. Charlie Mark spun on his heel and lunged forward. The impact of his body against the smooth, rock floor was like the clapping of two hands.

Jim Curry, with an exclamation of horror, ran forward. For the first time in his life he had aimed for his life. And now, he felt, he had killed his first man. He turned the limp body face uppermost. There in the exact center, and high up, was a crimson splotch. Curry turned hastily away and braced himself against the wall, sick at heart. The first death is a heavy burden on the brain and the heart.

He remained in that posture until his nerve returned and the tremor passed from him, but he was still weak when he went about the remaining work that had to be performed.

In the first place the horses must not be allowed to perish here in this subterranean stable. He loosed them, led them out through the entrance to the cave, and then gave them a sharp cut with his quirt to start them away toward freedom.

After that he came back and hesitated a moment over the body of the fallen man. To be sure, there had been nothing worth saving in the brain or the soul of this fellow, and yet the remorse and the horror of Jim Curry were hardly the less. Henry Mark, at least, would grieve for this extinguished life, and, for the sake of the old rancher, Jim Curry felt that he had taken a load of guilt upon his shoulders.

Should he bury the body outside under the stars? No, he had not time for that. Should he take the body back to the town and leave it where it might be found? No, because that would call up in the mind of Mark the belief that his adopted son had been murdered foully, and he would sanctify the memory of the outlaw and robber and man-killer. Better to leave him here where he had fallen.

With this conclusion the conqueror scooped up the money that still lay on the table with the firelight playing gently over it. He crammed it into his coat pocket and left the cave, carefully fitting back in place that large, thin, well-balanced stone that served as a door. Outside, he cast up a grateful glance to the bright, free stars, and then, swinging into the saddle on his uneasy horse, he touched it with the spurs and went rapidly down the gorge on the way to the home ranch.

He rode with a false sense of guilt, for in that

cave behind him, Charlie Mark was not dead. The bullet had made a grisly wound high on his forehead, a wound that seemed to show the entrance of the bullet to the brain, but, as a matter of fact, it had veered quickly upward in a course concealed by the growth of the hair. It was a deep wound, cutting a furrow in the skull, but it was by no means mortal. Stunned though he was, in the first moment of his half-recovered senses, Charlie Mark raised himself on one elbow and dragged himself to a corner of the cave where he pried up a flat stone and thrust his hand into the aperture beneath. Then he lay back with a grin of relief and triumph, for his fingers had closed over the precious rustling of paper money. Jim Curry had achieved only a half victory.

Besides, there would come another day. It was worth waiting for.

X

"You talk," said the sheriff, "like a gent that's been grievin' over a thing till he was plumb off his nut about it. I never heard such foolish talk, man."

He spoke with the calm of a very angry man who is controlling his anger only with the greatest difficulty. The flood of speech was

181

hardly dammed up behind his teeth. It was very early in the morning, besides—that time when even the best of men are apt to be a bit hostile even to their best friends. And as for the sheriff, he had not closed his eyes since he returned from the hunt that had given him—as guardian —the possession of Meg until she were sold at public auction. It had given him Meg, the peerless, but it had not brought to him any portion of the money, his own or that of Mrs. Carrigan. And the loss of the widow's money weighed more heavily on the heart of the honest sheriff than did the loss of his own. No wonder, then, that there was a touch of irritation in the voice of the sheriff as he answered the insinuation of the tall cowpuncher, Lang, that they ought to go to the Mark place and hunt for The Red Devil in his house.

But Lang insisted.

"I ain't saying for sure," he said. "I'm only saying that I'd like to have the search made. I ain't saying that him that robbed you last night, Sheriff, is the gent that's staying out at the Mark place. But I'm saying that they's sure something between them two. You come out there with me, and we'll take a look. If we don't find something . . . ."

"Well?" cried the sheriff. "What then?"

"If we don't find something," insisted Lang, coloring, "then I'm deaf and blind. I didn't see

182

the eyes of the gent that stuck me up . . . I didn't look at his frame . . . I didn't hear his voice, nor nothing."

"If you watched him particular close," said the sheriff, "you're the first gent I ever heard of that could see so many things accurate and hear so many things accurate when a hold-up artist had a gun on him, ready to talk business with powder and lead."

The tall man scowled blackly. "I could do that, and I could pull my gat and make a play for him, too," he said, and instinctively he touched the arm that had been wounded on the day of that hold-up as the penalty for daring to draw a weapon on The Red Devil.

The sheriff was moved in spite of himself. Beyond question Lang had showed nerve in plenty on that day, and a man who was willing to exchange shots with The Red Devil was a man for whom the sheriff could cherish a charitable share of patience.

"Suppose I go out there with you," he said, "will you shut your face after that about the man at the Mark place and stop bothering me?"

Lang swallowed. In his eye there was the yearning of the hound on the trail, but he assented.

The sheriff, accordingly, went out and down the steps at the rear of the house to get his horse. Lang accompanied him eagerly.

"We need something more'n just the hoss that you're going to ride on," insisted Lang. "We need the white mare . . . we need Meg."

"Eh?" said the sheriff. "Why do we need her?"

"Ain't it true," responded Lang, "that Meg and The Red Devil are pretty close to each other? Ain't it true that she comes when he whistles, and that she can pick him out of a crowd of a hundred?"

"Why, I dunno," said the sheriff noncommittally, although he began to take Lang more seriously from this moment, and showed it by a frowning side glance. "I dunno. Nobody ain't seen 'em much together, so far as I know. But, if you really think . . . well, Lang, confound you, we'll take Meg out and try your fool notion."

His tone, however, was much milder than his words, and there was even a touch of commendation in his manner as he escorted the taller man toward the corral.

In a few minutes they had saddled the sheriff's horse and Meg and led them out onto the road. They abandoned Lang's own mount, to wait for them at the hitching post, and struck out for the ranch of Henry Mark at a swinging gallop.

On the way they talked little. Lang kept his gaunt figure erect; only the compression of his lips and the glitter of his eyes showed that he felt an important crisis lay before them. And the sheriff began to grow more and more excited, and urged on Meg to greater and greater efforts as they neared the ranch.

And what a horse she was. The sheriff's own horse was a fine one, and Lang was horseman enough to show it to advantage. But Meg fairly floated over the road—head high, bright eyes gleaming kindly on all things around her, and this in spite of the hard ride of the day before. Both the sheriff and Lang marveled at her in silence.

"But don't it seem to you," said the sheriff, as they approached the ranch, "that it's kind of hard to trap The Red Devil . . . if the gent on Mark's place is really him or his partner . . . by his liking for the hoss or the liking of the hoss for him?"

"It ain't going to need the hoss altogether," replied Lang. "If it's The Red Devil, he'll have a hurt on his left hand or wrist. You seen the stains on Meg last night? We'll just hold her for luck. If his hand ain't hurt . . . well, then we're sure, anyway, that he didn't do the work last night. Afterward we can try him out on Meg, too. And if he gets by both tests, I'm willing to stop talking."

They were crunching the gravel of the road to the farmhouse underfoot now. Presently they had swung down—the sheriff from the mare and Lang from the sheriff's horse.

"We'll tether 'em here at this hitching rack around the corner of the house," suggested Lang. "That'll sort of take 'em by surprise."

It was done, and they then rapped at the door and were straightway admitted to the house by Ruth Mark.

"We dropped in to have a word with Jim," said the sheriff. "Might we see him, Ruth?"

"He's sleeping," said the girl. "He couldn't get much rest last night, I think. And no wonder. After that terrible man . . . but you tell them about it, Little Billy."

Billy, honored by this appeal to step into the limelight, at once accepted. He related how, coming back from their walk, they had seen the figure at the window and then the white horse under the trees, how Jim had cautioned him to be still and had gone alone—oh, thrilling act of courage!—into the house to find the bandit. And presently the bandit had rushed out on the far side of the house, whistled and called Meg to him, and disappeared without a single shot being sent after him. The whole number of grown men on the place at once rushed in pursuit and were gone for many hours down the valley, hunting for traces of the criminal. It was close to dawn when they came back and found that Jim was in bed. He admitted that he had stayed awake a good part of the night, and he now merely wished to be left alone and finish his nap.

His tale of the bandit was very simple. As he came upstairs, The Red Devil had slipped past and run down. That was all there was to it. His gun had stuck in the holster, and, before he could get it out for a shot in the darkness on the stairs, The Red Devil was by him and gone around a bend in the stairway.

"*Hmm,*" grunted the sheriff. "What you think of that, Lang?"

Lang was shaken, but he thrust out his jaw in determination.

"I want to talk to him," he said. "Let's go up."

The sheriff agreed, and they walked up the stairs, side-by-side. Ruth ran a few steps after them, whispering: "There's nothing wrong, Sheriff?"

"Sure there ain't, honey," said the sheriff. "We've just come to do a mite of talking. Go back and rest yourself."

At the door of the room above, the sheriff waved Lang to take the lead.

In the answer to the knock, they were not bidden to enter. Instead the door was opened, and to their surprise they saw Jim Curry before them, fully dressed. More than that, his left wrist was tightly bandaged, and Lang, in silence, pointed to it.

"Good Lord!" gasped out the sheriff.

His next act meant more than words. He shoved his long Colt under the nose of Jim.

"Stick up your hands," he said. "You're under arrest."

"Sure," said Jim coolly. "What's the charge?" he added as he raised the hands.

"Murder, robbery, and every other blamed thing in the calendar. Jim, you're under suspicion of being The Red Devil."

XI

A frightened cry from a girl, echoed by a boy's voice in the hall, warned them that they had been followed. Ruth and Little Billy stood there, white and incredulous.

"Take it all easy," said Jim reassuringly to them, although he himself had turned a little gray. "I'm going to show up this pair of four-flushers pretty *pronto*. Just rest easy, and . . . ."

"Save your talk," said the sheriff, "until you've told us how you come by that hurt on your left wrist. Fan him for a gun, Lang. All right. If you ain't got a gat on you, you can put your hands down, but I'm watching you, son, every minute."

"Follow me," said Jim Curry quietly. "Follow me, and I'll show you."

He led the group, now having added a panting, big-eyed Henry Mark, into the room across the hall and showed them the nail on the window sill on which he had torn his wrist. Instantly there was a chorus of approval and belief from Ruth and Little Billy and Henry Mark, but the sheriff insisted on having the wound unbandaged and examined. He was forced to admit that it was unlike the clean slash that a bullet would be apt to make, and now he turned to Lang for further guidance.

"Take him downstairs and outside," said Lang. "I got something to say to him in the open. But search his room first for the swag."

They combed the bedroom from top to bottom without revealing a sign of the needed money, and the sheriff consented at length to follow Lang's last suggestion, his gloomy face in no wise improved by the dignified tirade of Henry Mark.

"I'll hold this against you, sir," he was saying. "You have come under my roof to insult an honored guest, sir. And by the eternal, Sheriff Nance, I'll hold this against you to your death day, sir."

However, the family, including Little Billy, now jubilant and defiant, followed Jim Curry down the stairs and around the corner of the house where—to their surprise—they saw the sheriff's horse and near it the white form of Meg. There was no need to tell them what horse this was, for she had been described from fetlock to ear many and many a time; even had she not been described in detail, there was an air about her that often lingers about great horses, and it proclaimed great-hearted Meg as truly as the fragrance proclaims the rose.

But there was far more to hear and to see

immediately. No sooner did the beautiful mare see Jim Curry than she flung herself sheer back, snapped the rotten old halter rope like a bit of packing thread, and plunged straight for him. Before that rush the others gave back in a scurry, saw Meg slide to a halt on braced legs, and then rear straight up as though she would smash Jim Curry into the earth. Instead she came down with a whinny, and then she flirted at his hat with her nose while her great eyes gleamed with affection.

The others stood astonished, too astonished for speech or motion. Jim Curry glanced around him, and by the desperate glimmer of his eyes he seemed to be contemplating a break for freedom by leaping onto the back of the mare. Perspiration stood out on his forehead, but he did not make the move. The gun was still in the hand of the sheriff, and he would not be in too great a daze to whip it up and fire with deadly accuracy at the first sign of a flight. More than the sheriff, he saw in the face of Lang incredulous joy and exultation. The tall man was fairly gibbering with cruel pleasure. And even the Mark family, from Henry to Little Billy, stood back, white of face, for there was enough in the repute of The Red Devil to freeze the veins of anyone of them, no matter what kindness they had felt for him up to that time. Ruth herself stood back and veiled her eyes with her hands.

He was lost; plainly he was lost past hope. He was betrayed by the affection of his mare. Bitterly he touched her silken neck and stroked it mechanically while she nosed him in a frenzy of joy.

Then came one shrill note of faith, and it roused immense hope in Jim. It was the voice of Little Billy, trembling and broken with emotion.

"That don't mean nothing!" he was shrilling. "All hosses come pretty easy to Jim, and a pile of 'em will come running to him. They ain't no hoss that he's afraid of . . . and what does it mean if Meg comes to him?"

It was a feeble plea.

Lang took it up with a cruel sneer. "Then maybe he'd like to hop over the fence into the corral with that stallion yonder? Maybe he'd like to step inside the bars with the gray? That'd be proof he didn't fear nothing."

He pointed to the distant corral where the famous gray outlaw paced up and down, wolfish, and, as everyone knew, fierce as a wolf when he saw a chance to get at a man. Hero of a hundred horse-breaking contests, he had never yet been ridden, although one Jud Canby, two years before, had stayed four minutes on his back. But at length Jud had gone off like all the rest. They all fell. Moreover, they dared not let the wicked old stallion buck save on two ropes, so that he could be choked down and dragged away when he attempted to turn and crush the fallen rider. This was the beast to which Lang pointed, and Jim Curry knew the malice behind the gesture and knew, also, that he must accept the chance.

He made up his mind very quickly, as brave men do. He gave one glance about him, patted the neck of the mare again, heard the faint cry of horror from Ruth, and then turned on his heel. "Come along, boys," he said as cheerfully as he could. "I'll show you that Little Billy is right. There isn't a horse in the world that'll try to eat me. Old Bald Eagle ain't going to be any different from the rest."

Straight to the corral he marched, with the others following hastily, only Henry Mark lingering behind and urging Ruth to take the boy away to the house.

"It isn't going to be pretty," he was assuring his daughter.

"Are you going to allow this horrible murder . . . ?" Jim heard her saying, and then distance and the work before him swept all else from his mind.

Bald Eagle was a brute as scrawny and unlovely in outward appearance as he was terrible of heart within. He favored Jim with one narrow, side glance, and then halted in his uneasy walk and, dropping his head, pretended to be drowsing. That clumsy lure did not fool Jim Curry. He

192

hesitated, his hand freezing onto the rail on which it had fallen.

In that moment of suspense he was aware of the unplumbed blueness of heaven above him, of the whiteness of Meg in the distance, whinnying after him, of the bowed head of Ruth as the girl turned away. And at that he found the strength to slip between the bars and stand erect inside the corral—at the mercy of the stallion.

In a swirl of dust—so savage was his eagerness—the horse turned. There was a hoarse cry from the sheriff, repenting the brutal test to which he was submitting the man. Jim saw the revolver glint in the hand of Nance and blessed him for it. Then out shot the hand of Lang and knocked down the sheriff's arm.

"Let him finish," said Lang. "This ain't more'n what folks would do to him if he was brought into town and put in jail. No jail walls would keep him from the hands of them that wants to get at him."

But Bald Eagle was already upon him with terrible, snaky head outstretched, ears flattened, mouth agape. On toward him he tore—while Jim waited. One hope was with him—that the first onslaught would be so terrible that death would be instant. And he kept one belief—that afterward the girl would believe no wrong of him. Having seen him die dauntless, she would keep a shrine of faith for him in some part of her

193

being, no matter what tales the men of the world might bring up against him.

All of this rushed through his mind, for thought in that last second was plunging with the speed of traveling light. And so he saw Bald Eagle throw himself back, come to a sliding halt that cast a great, choking cloud of dust over him, and then there was the stallion rearing above him.

The great hoofs hung in the air—rushed down—and then swerved from the head at which they were aimed. An instant later Bald Eagle stood at a little distance, trembling, with his head held high, and shaking it in bewilderment at this man who neither cursed him nor beat him nor fled from him, but stood harmless, fearless, watching with the uncanny, human eyes. Bald Eagle snorted, then raised his head higher, pricked his ears, and neighed.

"By the eternal!" cried the sheriff. "Little Billy was right! Jim has a power over horses. Ruth, hold up your head and look, girl. I knew it all the time . . . in my heart. He's no more The Red Devil than I am. There he is . . . alive still, and he's done about the same thing with Bald Eagle as he did with Meg."

So thought the others. Even Lang was dull of eye, and watched Jim with a touch of horror as the latter left the corral. But there was no thought of retaliating for the malice the latter had shown him. Clambering through the bars of the corral, Jim Curry straightened and looked first of all to Ruth Mark, only to see her collapsing in the arms of her father. And then Little Billy ran at him, and he threw the youngster into the air, laughing hysterically, both of them, and white Meg came up and danced behind him for joy of that new meeting.

Lang drew back, evidently feeling that a hand of wrath was about to descend upon him, and the sheriff came up with his hand outstretched to Jim.

"I should've knowed," he said, "that a gent that could make horses come to him wasn't no man-killing hound. Will you shake hands and forget all about this, partner?"

Jim Curry took the hand with a crushing grip.

"Now," said the sheriff, "you go on to the house. I think that girl has something to say to you."

"And I," said Jim, still patting the neck of Meg, "have something to say to you. I'm not the man who robbed you, Sheriff, but suppose I showed you the money you lost. Do you suppose it might be arranged for me to have an inside track when it comes to the auctioning of Meg?"

The sheriff gasped. He turned white and then red in swift succession.

"You . . . ?" he muttered. "Does that mean . . . ?"

"It means," said Jim firmly, "that I'm not the man you want, Sheriff. Heaven strike me if I ever killed more'n one man in my life, and that man was a skunk that needed killing. Now what do you say about the bargain?"

"Bargain?" said the sheriff. "Why, son, it's a gift, not a bargain. Bad? Why, Jim, would The Red Devil make me a bargain like that? A fortune against one hoss?"

He caught the hand of Jim and wrung it, and Lang, beholding, turned his back and skulked hastily out of sight.

JIM CURRY'S SACRIFICE

I

Outside, the speed of the train blurred that indescribable desert, and, against that blur Charlie Mark, looking through the window, built up the pictures of his past. What he saw was not entirely pleasing. Certainly in the adopted rôle of bandit he had distinguished himself for a time at least. He left behind him a record of bloodshed and robbery that set his nerves tingling with a fierce scorn for his fellow men—and that made him look downward, lest someone in the train encounter one of those wolfish and hungry glances of contempt. In truth, as an amateur he had done very well indeed, and although he had been beaten—here he touched a scar in the center of his forehead running up into his hair—he had at least fought like a man, and only the greatest of the great had been able to bring him down.

Sufficient tribute to his cleverness was the fact that he was now riding in an eastbound train with his fellow citizens around him, and not a one of them suspicious of the fact that in the train with them was one who for two eventful months had carried upon his shoulders the character of The Red Devil, and in the rôle of that terrible and famous outlaw had committed enough deeds of villainy to pack the lives of ten ordinary criminals from birth to death. He sat among them. He ate with them in the diner. He chatted with them in the club car or on the observation car, and never a one of them could guess. And sometimes the exultation grew so great in Charlie Mark that his whole body shook in silent laughter as though an ague had gripped him. How utterly he despised these fools!

No matter if the real Red Devil, that strange man who had consented to change places with him in the beginning, had at length struck him down. No matter for that. He escaped miraculously with his life, and with enough money to set him up again in his interrupted career as a gambler in the East. That was his province, he felt. It was for the shrewd and deft work of cheating his fellows at cards that he had been born and placed upon this merry old earth. In his pocket was sufficient to pay the $20,000 in debts that had driven him from his old haunts. How they would be surprised when he appeared again! By this time they would have begun terming him a deadbeat. And now he would come to pay off all the debts at one sweep and still retain in his pocketbook the fat and tidy sum of $12,000.

$32,000 in two months—that had been his record. Why, this was better than Wall Street. A mask and a wig of red hair and a gun and a white horse had meant more to him than a handsome capital for investment. So greatly did the heart of the murderer and cardsharper rise in him that he turned his head from the window after a while and looked down the length of the car with a sort of lazy good-natured tolerance for the other men in it. They were sheep in his flock. Their fleece would eventually run through his hands, perhaps. All the world was filled with fools—and the fool's were working every day, hard, for the sake of the intelligent men, who, like himself, sat back and reaped the harvest of their labor.

The more he pondered it, the more he agreed with himself, and his eye became so gently inviting that a fellow passenger, wandering idly through the observation car in search of companionship and talk, settled into a neighboring armchair and turned half toward him with that vacuous eye and foolish smile that, as a rule, invites conversation.

Charlie Mark lounged a little about so as to face the stranger. The talk ran upon the desert, upon the weather, upon the speed of the train, upon the eternal curse of the sand that no window could exclude, even though it was close to stifling. Charlie Mark found it not difficult to keep up his end of the talk and at the same time look through and through the character of his companion.

He was a large and easy-natured man. His

hands were broad and thick, with the backs tanned and wind reddened, and the fingers square at the tip as though they had been blunted from surrounding the handle of a pitchfork on many a day and grinding into the hard base of his thumb. His clothes, too, were like the best suit of a farmer. The material was very good, but the fit was just a trifle snug, and the fashion was a full year stale. Assuredly Mr. Warner, as he gave his name, had increased in flesh and perhaps in prosperity, also—if the emerald stickpin were a sign—since that suit was tailored for him. He was not a fool, Charlie Mark decided. His black eyes were keenly focused. The movements of his head, even on the burly neck, were quick and decisive. He was readily moved to laughter, but only when he was honestly amused. He was by no means one of those idiots who burst into tides of laughter to accommodate a neighbor.

On the whole he struck Charlie Mark as a man proud of his own opinion, shrewd in a bargain, and fond of maintaining his superiority and his sense of superiority with those with whom he had dealings. Charlie Mark observed him with a growing animation of the spirit. Such a fellow as this might yield many a handful of fine feathers at a plucking.

Instinctively Charlie Mark flexed his fingers a few times and rejoiced to find that gun work had not appreciably stiffened them, although they were far indeed from the matchless adroitness that they had attained before he left his haunts in the East for this singular trip into his own Western country.

He had grown a trifle absent-minded in the course of these reflections. Mr. Warner nodded somewhat stiffly to a tall, gaunt man in passing, and immediately, when the tall man's back was turned, he cast a significant glance toward Charlie Mark. The latter nodded his handsome head and waited attentively.

"Know him?" asked Warner.

"I don't."

"You've heard of him, anyway. That's John Cameron Butler. He's the one that owns the company that turns out the J.C.B. plows. I guess that places him for you?"

He looked expectantly at Charlie Mark after the fashion of one waiting to see surprise registered. Charlie Mark allowed himself to exhibit a proper degree of surprise, although he had never heard of either Butler or his plows before that moment.

"Yes, sir," rambled on Warner, lost in admiration of the broad, convex back of the great man as he settled down on the observation platform. "Yes, sir . . . that's old J.C. Butler. He's got the plow that scratches most of the surface of Kansas and Nebraska already, and he's spreading north and south mighty fast. The shares of his plow have a great throw to 'em. That's one of their big talking points. And then they have a queer angle of taking the ground . . . that counts too. Anyway, that's J.C.B. He's got his initials stamped into about a million plowshares by this time, I guess. Yes . . . or more than that." He paused. "And I went to the same school with him," he concluded.

Charlie Mark was properly astonished.

"Yes, sir, I went to the same school with him," continued Warner. "And we studied the same books, even if we didn't learn the same things out of 'em. I didn't see much about plows." He chuckled at this ghost of a jest. "At that, I learned enough to do pretty well. But I guess they forgot to write in books just how a man can make money when he gets out of school. Wonder why they leave it out, Mister Mark?"

Charlie smiled in turn.

"Not that I'd like to be the same kind that J.C.B. is, for all his money. He's so set in his ways that nobody can tell him a thing . . . not a thing! He knows what he knows, and nobody can shake him. Take cards, for instance. He's never lost a game of cards in his life, he says, so long as he's playing for money."

"What?" exclaimed Charlie Mark, startled out of character by the suddenness with which the talk had turned to the mysteries of his own calling. "Never lost a game of cards?"

204

"Not when he's gambling."

"Hmm," said Charlie Mark, and then settled back in his chair and tucked his chin deep in the bosom of his coat and regarded the slim tips of his folded fingers.

Was it possible that there were upon the earth such idiots as J.C. Butler and his credulous friend? No, it could not be true, and yet Mr. Warner continued.

"He trimmed me bad last night, and this morning he did the thing over again. He sits back there in his drawing room like a king on a throne and just pities anybody that has the nerve to play with him." Mr. Warner gritted his teeth. Plainly he did not like to recall the game in which evidently he had lost a great deal of money. "For my part," he declared, "I'd go a long way to trim him, even if I had to do it with a trick and tell him about it later on when I sent the money back."

Charlie Mark turned in his chair. This sounded like the baldest and most stupid and crassest advance agent work for a crooked gambler that he had ever heard. But his glance included, again, the brown-red hands of Warner, and the large emerald stickpin. And his suspicions subsided. This could not be a frame-up. The weather stains ingrained in the seams along this man's forefinger must be real. He half closed his eyes and reviewed his own appearance. No, there

205

could be nothing in his own appearance that would make him seem to be a man carrying a large sum of money.

Opening his eyes again, he said: "How could you trim him? What's the trick?"

"It needs two," confessed Warner.

Again Charlie Mark turned and stared, and again Warner met him with a bland eye. No, this could not be crooked. It was too old for that. It was all stuff twenty years old at least.

"Go on," said Charlie Mark.

"This way," explained Warner, and briefly he outlined his scheme. It was to enter into talk with the great man of the plow, get him into a stud poker game—the only kind Butler played, it seemed—and then trap him.

"I'll sit beside him," explained Warner, "because when he lifts his under card, he always lifts it pretty hard, and I can see what it is. Every time I can tell you what that card is. The thing to do is to wait until he bluffs, and then call him. He'll start betting high all at once when maybe he's away under a good hand. He'll bet so high that he backs a man down . . . . That's the way he cleans up most of the time. He plays to one big hand, and, when he's won that, he stops and nothing can make him play any more."

"A short sport, eh?" murmured Charlie Mark. And he sighed as he looked at his traveling companion. It was too easy and too good to be true—far too good.

What followed was like a dream, it was so simple. With $32,000 in his pocket, and perhaps $1,000,000 to the bank account of the man who he was to face—was it not perfect? In half an hour they were settling down in the drawing room of the large and prosperous Mr. Butler with the last whisper of Warner still running pleasantly in the ear of Charlie Mark.

"You'd better let me give you some money, because Butler is apt to go to the sky if you try to call his bluff. Let me give you something to . . . ."

"I have enough," said Charlie Mark, controlling his smile. "I think I can manage. Never mind your help."

Why should he share with an accomplice like this? If he borrowed a stake to play with, he must split according to the proportion of the loan compared with his own capital.

"It will be a joke, eh?" Warner chuckled. "We'll have the laugh on him when we give back his money, eh? And we won't give it back till the train gets in."

Charlie Mark agreed with a smile. Restore the money? He laughed internally again. Truly the fools were not all dead.

The game was even simpler than the approaches to it. The great goddess Fortune favored him absurdly. He had to cheat in his deals in order to lose, instead of win. And always there was the inevitable Warner sitting snugly in the corner of the seat beside the fat Butler, and signaling the buried card infallibly every time it fell. He was enjoying the game like a great child.

But as time went on, Warner began to grow worried. He seemed to fear that something had gone wrong with Mr. Mark. And when Butler was called out of his room for a moment by a train acquaintance with a black cigar and an ancient jest, Warner confided his worries.

"He's liable to run 'em up high any hand now," he protested. "You'd better start winning."

"Don't trouble about me," said Charlie Mark. "I'm trailing the old sport like a foxhound. He's getting the taste. After a while I'll trim him a little. Then he'll come with a strong bluff, and I'll raise him to the skies. Watch it work."

Warner was still protesting when Butler came back.

The game proceeded exactly as Charlie Mark had prophesied. Shortly after the return of his host, he trimmed the man of the plows for four thousand at a stroke, a loss that put Butler back even with the game and clouded his brow so that Warner signaled to Charlie Mark that the blow would probably come immediately.

And it came. It was on Charlie Mark's deal. He sent slipping across the table a buried card that Warner immediately signaled as a jack. And no sooner had another jack gone on its way to Butler than that worthy immediately bet $1,000. Betting had been high, but such betting as this was thrilling even to the case-hardened nerves of such a professional gambler as Charlie Mark. He covered that $1,000.

He was dealing with skill as great as he had ever shown before. In his delight over his own command of the pack, he determined to make the hand a close one. And it seemed to Charlie Mark, so adroitly was he manipulating the cards that the pack was responding to his bald wishes rather than to the cunning work of his fingers. He was reading them three down as he dealt. He was burying them under the bottom every lick. He thrilled with his own sense of prowess. After all, next to the joy of shoving a revolver under the chin of a man, there was nothing like tying him up in a crooked bit of work at a card table.

Now he was drawing it with a fine edge. He sent to Butler—who was betting an even thousand with every card that came his way—another jack and two aces—a jack full on aces, which ought to be enough, considering the way the cards were running, to make the older man bet his head off. To himself, with consummate and tantalizing skill, he gave two queens on top of a buried queen and two tens. Would Butler buck that combination with a hair-raising bluff? In the meantime, Warner was leaning forward, perspiring with anxiety, and only drew a long breath of relief and settled back when he received the signal that the buried card was a queen. A queen full over a jack full—that ought to satisfy old Butler when he was called.

The bluff came immediately. Old Butler studied the cards almost at once, and then—with a set jaw that betrayed his state of mind as clearly as though he had stated it in typewriting—he raked out his wallet, he produced a checkbook from it, and he inscribed the letters with wide, blunt strokes of ink—$20,000! Slowly, with incredulous eyes, Charlie Mark saw that sum written down and then the signature planted at the bottom of the check.

After all, was not this more thrilling than any hold-up, even though there were less of an element of danger in it?

"Twenty thousand!" cried the man of the plow. "Twenty thousand, sir. That is how sure I am that my hand is better than yours!"

Charlie Mark looked into that expanding, swollen countenance for a moment. Then, fearful of betraying himself with a grin, he looked hastily down again. He in turn produced a wallet. His fingers, in spite of himself, shook a little with pleasure as he counted out in bills the sum of $20,000—twenty bills of $1,000 each, and then, in a separate stack, $8,000 more in cash, also—all that he had. Would to heaven that he had had more with him—a hundred thousand more!

"See that twenty," he said carelessly, pushing the money forward, "and raise you eight."

No, it was well he had bet no more than the eight. Mr. Butler regarded the money with intent eyes. Then he slowly drew out the checkbook again and wrote down the exact amount and no more. Plainly he was hesitant about risking another lump sum. But he managed to finish the check and pushed it out.

"Call you, sir," he said, frowning in doubt.

Warner, leaning forward, his broad fat face shining with perspiration, seemed unable to breathe with ease.

Charlie Mark pushed back his chair a little and shifted in it so that his automatic would be more readily under his hand. One could never tell when there would be gun play in this part of the country. If so, he would be ready for it—and heaven help Mr. Butler if he attempted to resent with a slug of lead the departure of thirty thousand and some odd dollars.

Then slowly Charlie Mark drew the buried queen toward him, raised it, studied the face of the lady an instant, and deposited it gently on the surface of the table beside the rest of his hand. "A queen full," he said mildly to Butler.

"Eh?" grunted the other. "A queen full?" He jerked his glasses away from his nose and leaned far forward as though he must now verify the truth with the naked eye. "A queen full!" he gasped out at length. "Right you are. A queen full." He leaned back.

A thrill of pity ran through Charlie Mark. After all, the simple old fellow was going to take defeat like a gamester.

"Not quite good enough, though," was what the man of the J.C.B. plow was saying.

Could Charlie Mark credit what his ears told him?

"Not quite good enough, my boy."

And the fat hand turned over the buried card —not the jack that Charlie expected, but, to his horrified eyes, there was exposed one black spot in an expanse of shining white—the fatal ace of spades!

It was literally like a physical shock. The blow struck him somewhere in the base of the brain and kept him bowed and staring for a long moment. Then he straightened and found that Mr. Warner, that simple Mr. Warner was watching him with a hard and cynical smile of derision.

He had been done. He had been done like the simplest and most idiotic gull in the world. Blackness swam across his eyes. No, there must be no killing, simply because there was no escape from a train speeding along at the rate of sixty miles an hour. He had been trimmed, and he must wait for a chance to revenge himself.

What were they saying?

"You ought to give up cards and go in for plows, Mister Mark. I'm sure I can make a place for you in my factory."

Charlie Mark turned on them a white and terrible smile, then stumbled out of the drawing room and into the buzzing aisle beyond.

II

They had not passed the confines of the desert. No, the blank, broad miles of sand still stretched out toward the horizon, and beyond the horizon edge was the pale shimmer of the heat waves rushing up into the sky.

And Charlie Mark had thought to take plunder out of this terrible land and deliver it in the East. The whole thing seemed ridiculous for a moment. No, there was only one way, and that was to live in the West—as a strictly, stupidly law-abiding citizen, or else to live in the West as a man destroyer, tearing their winnings from the hands of others. The latter was the rôle that he preferred.

But what was he to do now? He could not face the East. The debts he owed there would destroy him and his game, he foresaw. There was only one thing, and that was to go back to the West again, go back either as The Red Devil, under which grim name he had carved his place as an outlaw, or else go back to his adopted father's house and there attempt to wheedle the old man out of sufficient money to pay off those gambling debts.

If that failed, there remained another trip on the road as The Red Devil. And once he was back on his feet—oh, to have it in his power to reach this Warner and his friend Butler. The agonizing part of it was that the very simplicity and age of their ruse could so completely have blinded his eyes.

But with $10 in his pocket, he must first of all leave this train at the first stop and trust to luck that he would be guided once again into the path of Warner and Butler so that he might add something to their account that would strike a balance.

The first stop proved to be little more than a water tank and section house, but it was a point where Charlie Mark could catch a train running West. Before the afternoon had begun, he was bumping westward on a slow freight to the ruin of his most presentable suit of clothes.

That journey was among the most grisly memories of Charlie Mark. He could figure very effectively as a man-killer or a gambler in polite circles, but between these two extremes he was not at home, and particularly as a hobo working the freights, he was by no means a success. He lost his last bit of money and his suitcase on the same night, due to the ministrations of a friendly hobo who he had helped the day before. And at length he was forced to drop off the train at a small town and pick up a few square meals by dint of battering doors. And all the while he could only pray that the unshaven whiskers would effectually mask his face and keep him from being recognized, for now he was approaching his home district in the mountains.

Scarcely a hundred miles away, he found an opportunity to lift a wallet from a cowpuncher in a village street, and with that wallet he was able to buy enough articles to make up a bundle, and so he arrived again at the home town of Hampton. Avoiding the town proper, he struck out across country for the house of his adopted father.

In that last stretch he summed up his position accurately. First of all, he must get Jim Curry out of the household of the Mark family. He looked upon that formidable individual with a mixture of hatred, fear, and admiration. And in justice to himself, it must be admitted that the fear had nothing to do with the prowess of Jim Curry with a gun. It was based entirely upon a superstitious sense that told Charlie Mark that fate was at work on his destiny, and against fate it did not avail to use every scruple of his wit and cunning.

Look at it as he would, it seemed that it was fate that had determined to reclaim the outlaw, Jim Curry, who had terrorized the mountain desert under the name of The Red Devil, and for five of six years had escaped retribution through his own prowess and the speed of his white mare, Meg. Fate had determined to reclaim him, and therefore Charlie Mark had been tempted, picked up like a pawn, and thrust into the place that the removal of Curry left vacant. And to make the exchange perfect and polished in every respect, the first resting place that Curry had found, after he gave up his lawless life and attempted to fit into the ways of civilized man, was in the former home of Charlie Mark.

Look at it as he might, there was no manner in which the phenomenal could be removed from these events. A strange force was pushing Charlie Mark in one direction and Jim Curry in the other. And a dim perception that his soul was being damned while the soul of Curry was being saved enraged Charlie Mark to the core of his heart.

How else had his flight toward the East been stopped by those two simple, and simply crafty, criminals who went under the names of Warner and J.C. Butler, of plowing fame?

Revolving these thoughts in a gloomy mind, Charlie Mark approached the house of Henry Mark. He did not go directly to the door. Since

216

his brief career as The Red Devil, it had become impossible for him to approach any house directly without first skirting about it and trying, if possible, to examine into the number and nature of the men within its walls.

He slipped to the side of the rambling old house, walked noiselessly along the side of the verandah—keeping very close to the wall by instinct, so that he would make no sound—and came at length to the windows that overlooked the front room, the parlor.

There, as he had expected, he found them. And there was enough food for thought in what he saw to keep him crouched, long, at the window, examining them face by face and gesture by gesture.

First of all, there was his adopted father, that good old man who in all the length of a life among hard men and in hard times had never been known to do an ungenerous thing or take an unfair advantage or to act in any manner other than as a benevolent well-wisher to all around him. And like many a kindly man was as grim as his heart was gentle. Beetling white brows covered his eyes, and the cut of his jaw was the square type that from time immemorial has designated the fighter. And fighter, indeed, he was, as all knew who met him in fair battle.

He was lying on a couch now in a corner of the room with his back and shoulders supported and partly propped up by a mass of pillows, while his work and time-hardened hands were folded behind his head. His eyes were closed, but he was not asleep. Instead, his lips parted from time to time, and, although Charlie Mark heard nothing because of the humming of the wind about his ears and the thickness of the wall between, he made out that the old man was answering the puzzled queries of young Billy, that nameless and homeless little vagrant who had been included in the home circle by the far-reaching arm of Henry Mark.

Little Billy sat now at a table by the side of the room and near the couch of the master of the house. Here he puzzled over his book, preparing lessons for the next day's school. Lessons were hard for Little Billy, as Charlie Mark remembered from the old days, but in those times the youngster had been compelled to do his studying in the loneliness of his own room. Since that time, two short months ago, some softening influence had entered the house and broken down the bars.

That influence was not far to be sought. The sound of the piano, rising clear as the wind fell away in its whining, now died out altogether, and Charlie Mark was able, by moving a little at the window, to see the piano itself at the far end of the big room—also the group at it. There were only two in that group—his sister, by adoption,

Ruth Mark, she who had ever seen through his pleasant exterior and into the hardness and the cruel cunning of his inner heart, and beside her was the man of men—Jim Curry now, The Red Devil of old.

Upon these two Charlie Mark stared, forgetting time and forgetting caution, pressing his face close to the windowpane. It was not difficult to see that Ruth and Jim were profoundly interested in each other. He was leaning close to her, talking earnestly, his lean face suffused with color, his eyes lighted. Perhaps he was praising the music she had finished playing. But now she raised a hand in protest and laughed. He could only see her in profile, but that was enough. There was a moist light in her eye, an uncertainty about her smile that spoke eloquent volumes.

Was he in love with her? Perhaps so, and perhaps not. He was the one man who Charlie Mark would not pretend to read at a glance. Was she in love with him? To that question there was only one answer—she was profoundly in love. And Charlie, remembering the many men who had come courting in the past, and remembering how they had always been received with a careless lightness, was now the more impressed.

But one thing stood out firmly in his mind: Jim Curry, the former outlaw, was imbedded in the family circle of the Marks like a rock in its natural foundation. And it must be his work to uproot him and throw him out of his place of pleasant security. Why? Because he dared not and would not live with, facing under the same roof, a man who knew the truth about him, and such a man was Jim Curry.

That conviction was hardening in his heart, and he was already casting about for the first hint of a plan on which he could afterward act, when, behind him, a small, quiet voice said: "You've come sneaking back at last, eh?"

III

He started up, flushing with shame and anger to be caught in this wretched position as a spy on the quiet household, and the eyes that his eyes met were those of Little Billy. Doubtless, he had pressed so close to the glass of the window that he had made some noise and had attracted the furtive attention of the child. He could only be grateful that Little Billy had not, as most spiteful children would have done, called the attention of the entire family to the presence of the spy at the window.

"Hello, Little Billy," said Charlie Mark, smoothing over the unfriendly greeting of the child. "I'm mighty glad to see you again."

"Glad nothing," snorted Little Billy.

There was so much maturity in the brief scorn

of this answer that Charlie Mark blinked in amazement.

"Look here," he said, "how do you come to talk like this to me?"

"I saw you there," said Little Billy, and pointed toward the window in front of which Charlie had been kneeling.

"I was taking a look at the folks. I wanted to see what they looked like when I came back. So I stole a look through the window, Little Billy. That's all."

There was another grunt from Little Billy. "I seen the side of your face," he said.

"What d'you mean by that?" asked Charlie, increasingly angered by this continued attack.

"Well," exclaimed Little Billy by implication, "once I seen the side of a coyote's head when it came sneaking around the chicken yard in the moonlight! You looked the same way . . . only worse. And I'll bet my new rifle that you've come back for the same reason . . . you want to steal something away!"

"You little brat!" cried Charlie Mark.

To his speechless astonishment, Little Billy, who had always hated him, but who had at least had the grace to shrink from his path and give him the right of way—this same child now refused to budge an inch. Stare for stare he repaid Charlie Mark. And the hand of Charlie dropped to his side. He could not speak for a moment.

"What devil is in you?" he asked when his breath had returned. "You little dirty-faced . . . ."

"Shut up," broke in Little Billy. "You can't cuss me, and you can't beat me up. It can't be done by nobody the size of you."

"No?" Charlie Mark sneered. "I see that you've been running amuck since I left. It's time that you were taken in hand, Little Billy, and by the gods I'm the man to do it."

"Are you?" said the astonishing Little Billy, still refusing to give way a single pace. "I tell you what, Charlie . . . if you hit me, even with your open hand, you'll be sorry for it as long as you live."

Curiosity was greater than rage in Charlie Mark. He mastered the latter long enough to inquire: "How do you make that out, son?"

"If you seen what happened last week, you'd know why," said Billy. "You remember big Tucker . . . Jerry Tucker?"

"Of course I do."

"I give his kid brother a good licking at school, and Joe Tucker went right home and told Jerry that I'd licked him with a club instead of fighting fair. So Jerry came out, got me, and sure polished me off." Little Billy chuckled as he touched his still discolored eye. "He cleaned me up," continued the boy, "and, when I came inside the house, the first one to see me was Jim. He didn't wait. He asked about two questions. Then he started." Little Billy stopped, breathing hard.

"Go on," said Charlie Mark, and called up the memory of Jerry Tucker, vast of shoulder, proved in courage.

"I seen it through the window!" cried Little Billy. "My eyes was swelling shut, but I held 'em open so's I could watch. My, Jim was like a . . . a tiger. He just ate Jerry Tucker up . . . beat him till it made me sick to see it . . . and finally I ran out and begged him to stop. Jerry got up then, and staggered away. But his face was like a slice of beefsteak."

"And I'll get the same if I touch you, eh?"

"Jim told me to mind my business," said Little Billy. "But if anybody bigger'n me hurts me, I'm to come tell him. And you better watch out, Charlie. I ain't going to take a single step back for you . . . or ten like you . . . not while I got a real, honest Injun man like Jim around to back me up."

Charlie Mark regarded the child for a sober moment. This was far unlike the cringing fear of the Little Billy he remembered. Truly a sweeping change had come over the household, and Billy's attitude was significant of it.

"Jim put you up to this, eh? Well, I'll settle that with Jim. He told you to get ready for me the minute I came back, and then start in on me? He told you to talk like this?"

"Jim don't have to tell me what to say," said the boy proudly. "Neither do you. But I'll tell you one thing, Charlie. You keep shy of Jim, or he'll run over you like a tornado. I've seen him at work, and I know."

He turned and sauntered toward the front door from which he had come, and Charlie Mark followed. But first, in the shadow of the verandah roof, he furtively and instinctively raised his right hand and touched the scar on his forehead. It was true, he reflected. Jim Curry was a tiger. His claws must be trimmed before he was ejected from the house.

In the meantime, was this talk of Little Billy's a specimen of how he was to be received in the household? Little Billy and Ruth, he knew, had always seen or guessed at the truth about his sinister and hidden nature. Had they spread the poison to Henry Mark, or did that stanch anchor still hold?

They were through the door. They crossed the hall. They entered the parlor, with Little Billy saying curtly: "Look what I found peeking through the window."

And instantly the doubts of Charlie were dissolved. Henry Mark came from the couch at the first sound of the voice of his adopted son. He whirled, his long arms flew out, and he caught Charlie in a great embrace.

Very strange was that exhibit of emotion from

Henry Mark. Never in his life had Charlie seen the equal of it, but the explanation was quickly forthcoming.

"I've been thinking of you, Charlie," cried the older man, "as though you was a goner . . . as though you was as plumb gone as if a ship had been sunk and you'd gone down with her. I've given you up, Son. And now that you come . . . why, dog-gone me if it don't strike me all of a heap."

His color, indeed, had changed as he spoke. Charlie Mark felt that body, gaunt with age, grow weak and tremble in every limb. Carefully he lowered the other back to the couch, while Ruth Mark came with a cry.

There was fire in her eye as she struck away his hands.

"Always to do some harm!" she cried at him. "That's always why you come. And the minute you enter the house, trouble enters with you. Oh, I wish that you'd stayed where you were!"

"Hush up, child," whispered her father faintly. "I'm feeling better already. It was just that . . . just that my breath was sort of took short, Ruth . . . you know?"

In the meantime, Charlie Mark employed an infinitesimal fraction of a second to glance at Jim Curry. That glance was all he needed. A strange mixture of scorn, disgust, hatred, and fighting rage showed in the eye of the ex-outlaw as he looked at Charlie, but in an instant his eye turned with alarm and concern on the face of Henry Mark.

It was enough to give Charlie insight into an unsuspected strength—Jim Curry was devoted to the man who had taken him in. And the strength of that devotion would secure him, Charlie Mark, from the dangerous anger of the gunfighter.

He had no chance to explain further. The old man was himself again, sitting up and pouring forth a volley of questions. He answered them as well as he could. It was desire to see the mountains that had induced him to postpone his return home. And now he had seen them to his heart's content. Where had he been in them? Well, that was a long story. He would tell it by degrees—stories of everything from mountain climbing to hunting.

And he meant what he said. He needed only time in which to invent the details. Then he would talk of everything, except the truth of his time spent as a bandit. And as he spoke, he raised his eyes and exchanged glances with Jim Curry.

He saw that the girl had gone back to Jim as to a natural shelter in a time of storm. Close beside him, she looked anxiously back at her father and the adopted son.

"But what are you standing there for, girl?" cried her father at length. "Are you blind? Don't you see who it is? Don't you see that it's our Charlie come back to us? Eh? And come back to stay, lad . . . tell me that . . . that you've come back to stay!"

"Heaven willing," answered the hypocrite. "The one thing I want to do, Father, is to spend the rest of my life here with you."

"You hear, Ruth?" cried the old man. "You hear what he says? Why I'm glad that he's stayed away so long, if it needed that stay to teach him this. But now stir into the kitchen, girl, and bring out something . . . a snack for our Charlie. Lord, it'll do my heart good to see you eating my food under my roof once more, lad."

And he struck Charlie on the shoulder again and again in an ecstasy of pleasure. Certainly it was a strange manner in which to greet a youth not of his own kin, but, adopted before a child was born in the house of Henry Mark, Charlie had always been treated like an actual son, and even with greater affection than Ruth herself received.

She hurried out of the room to execute the mission in the kitchen, and the old man now took the arm of Charlie through his own and advanced smilingly toward Jim Curry, who had by this time mastered his scowl of distaste and had even forced a faint smile upon his clean-cut features.

"Here," said Henry Mark, "is a man I want you

to know and learn to understand like he was your brother, Charlie. This is Jim. What his other name is, I dunno. But names don't count. But I want you boys to get to know each other, Charlie. I'm counting on Jim to teach you to love the West."

They came closer. They shook hands in silence. And both of them knew that the great battle for mastery had commenced.

IV

While their hands closed one over the other, the bitter realization grew in Charlie Mark that the former outlaw, Jim Curry, or plain Jim as he called himself here, was a better man than he. And his soul shrank with that knowledge and grew hard with hatred. Yes, the greeting that he had received from Little Billy had been, after all, significant of a change in the household. Three enemies were now housed under that roof, and his only friend was old Henry Mark himself. But would not the other three succeed in poisoning the old man against him? Little Billy stood off in a corner, glancing from time to time at Jim as though asking for directions, and then again scowling at Charlie Mark and chewing his nether lip like a much larger and older man filled full of bewilderment and anger.

After a short time Ruth returned carrying a tray that, in her eagerness to get back to the scene of the fray, she had filled with food at lightning speed. The small, round table in the center of the room was covered with the articles she brought—thick-grained, homemade bread cut in even slices for all her haste, as Charlie noted, slabs of cold roast beef, and marmalade dense with crowded half-moons of orange peel. Besides, there were numerous little dishes taken out of the cooler. The very sight of them recalled to Charlie Mark the memory of that cooler—the old frame under the fig tree, covered with thick sacking, and on top of it a tub that by means of wet clothes dripped constantly over the sacking all the day. He recalled that cooler, and many a hot day when he and Ruth had come in from the sunshine, all overheated with play, and how often he had pillaged that cooler of its store of cool milk and cider, and shared that pillage with the little girl.

Did she remember those days now? He looked up and saw that her eye, as she watched him eat, had grown larger and softer, but the moment her glance crossed his, her face hardened again. Plainly his cause was lost, so far as she was concerned, forever. And it hurt him more than he cared to admit, even to himself. He looked quickly away, and his eyes found a resting place on the delighted face of Henry Mark. Truly he could not have been more pleased if a son of his own had returned.

The rest of that evening passed in a blur for Charlie Mark. He knew afterward that a stream of questions had been poured on him, and that he had parried them as fast as he could, promising full replies on the morrow, until he escaped with a plea of weariness, also that old Henry Mark himself helped him up the stairs to his room. When the door closed and he was left alone, he sank down on the side of the bed and brooded bitterly on himself and his situation.

He had been moving so rapidly through the wild scenes of the past weeks that he had had small time to think them over. Now, in his old home, with memories of a former life, an innocent and harmless life, stirring around him, the sense of guilt came heavily upon him. So the moments ran like running sand, one into the other, and extended to hours; still he sat there although the lamp, running low in oil, was beginning to sputter. Indistinctly he had heard the sounds of people climbing the stairs and going to bed— that was long before—and voices had called to him wishing him a sound sleep. But now came a single stealthy tap at the door.

He knew at once that Jim Curry was waiting for him in the hall. First he looked to his revolver. Then he opened the door. He found the outlaw there, as negligent in attitude as ever, and as careless in his manner, although Charlie Mark knew that every moment he was being watched as a cat watches the mouse nearing its hole and safety.

"Well?" queried Charlie Mark.

"Seems to me," answered Jim Curry, "that the questions ought to come from my side and the answers from yours. You're living . . . and yet I've thought you were planted permanent up yonder in the cave."

"Sure you did," snarled Charlie Mark, "and you're sorry that I'm not there."

"I am," answered Jim Curry, "except that I don't like to have a killing on my hands . . . even if it is the killing of a rat like you."

Charlie Mark nodded slowly in the darkness. "You're trying to start something like a fight, Jim, even here in my own house?"

"Your own house?" Jim Curry sneered. "It's more mine than yours, by right."

"I knew you'd be figuring it that way before long."

"Charlie, tell me straight . . . have you got a spark of affection for a single person in this house?"

"Bah," muttered Charlie Mark. "This kind o' talk makes me sick. What do you want with me, Curry?"

"I want to tell you this . . . either you or I

have to leave this here house, and have to leave *pronto*. Understand?"

"Of course I understand. But do you ever imagine that Henry Mark will let me go?"

"That's the trouble," admitted Jim Curry. "But the girl and I both figure he'd be happier. . . ."

"You've told the girl?" whispered Charlie in fury. "You've been filling her ears with talk about me?"

"I don't need to," said Jim Curry. "She knows every angle of your nasty soul like a book."

"Well," said Charlie, "I've played a lone hand more than once before, and I can play it again and do fairly well, I think, at that."

There was a pause. It seemed that Jim Curry was debating in his mind whether or not it might be worth his while to continue the argument. Eventually he said only: "I follow your drift, son. You want to make it a fight from the start. Well, that suits me. But I'm going to give you one piece of advice . . . not for your own sake, but because I hate to have the old man's heart broke by finding out what sort of a skunk you are. My advice is for you to take off that fob you're wearing and throw it away."

"Thanks," said Charlie Mark. "You want me to throw it your way, I guess?"

The fob to which Jim had called attention was solid gold.

232

"You probably stole it, Charlie. And if you did, you're a fool for wearing stolen goods."

"Am I? Why?"

"You never can tell when somebody will come along . . . somebody that'll recognize what you have."

"You talk like a fool, Curry. This fob is the same as a million others. It's just a nugget beat out flat and round. Nothing queer about it. Besides, the fellow who owned it is not at all likely to come around and ask questions about the fob."

"One of those you killed, eh?"

"Never mind about that. You make me sick inside and out and all the way through, Curry, with your talk . . . as if you never shot a man."

"Never to kill . . . except when I shot at you. And luck saved you that time . . . worse luck for me. Maybe there'll be another time, though, Charlie. And you can lay to this . . . if you start any cussedness around here and disgrace your father and Ruth, I'm coming after you, son, and I'll give you a worse hunting than any sheriff and his posse would do. Don't forget it."

"Thanks," answered Charlie Mark, grinding his teeth with anger. "And take this in exchange. You can't steal the girl, Jim. It can't be done. You can't get Ruth."

"You fool," breathed Curry. "Do you think I am as high as Ruth?"

"Keep it under your hat," said Charlie Mark, chuckling. "If you're half as good a man as you pretend, you'll never dream of asking her to marry you. Because after you were married, what if someone popped up with the right dope on what you used to be? What would become of your family . . . what would become of Ruth, Jim?"

Jim Curry leaped for his tormentor, but the door was slammed heavily in his face, and he recoiled with a groan into the darkness of the hallway.

V

It would not have been hard to tell which of the two had gained the victory in that first wordy encounter. Charlie Mark turned back into his room, chuckling through his set teeth—with a strange mixture of rage and satisfaction as he recalled the insults he had been forced to countenance, and the poisonous thrust that he had at length managed to deal to his enemy.

Jim Curry, on the other hand, did not close his eyes for half the night, but sat with his head in his hands on the side of his bed, recalling the last words Charlie Mark had spoken.

Were they true? At least they had acted as a sharp check to him. They brought him up short and made him think suddenly of all phases of the question. Where was he drifting with Ruth Mark? What was the meaning underneath all of the happy hours that they were spending together more and more as the days drew on? Why was he staying at the Mark place, above all? What right had he there, or what claim had he upon Henry Mark, except his honest affection for the old man, for the girl, and for Little Billy, not the least of all? But here he was idly drifting and waiting, it seemed, for something to happen.

Had Charlie Mark been right? Was he indeed heading straight toward a love affair with Ruth? Was it already so obvious that a new arrival, like Charlie Mark, could tell at the first glance how matters stood? It shamed him, and yet it thrilled him. If this were true, then at least it meant that she was not showing indifference, to say the least.

But, after all, was not Charlie right? To let matters drift on would be the height of dishonesty, would be the truest way, indeed, of inviting disaster later on—disaster that would involve not only himself, but the girl, also.

He thought back to his past, just as Charlie Mark had done the night before, but with how different an emotion. Outlaw and bandit he had been, but he had been forced from the pale of law in the first place through no fault of his own, but by the exigencies of chance, and, if he had lived by plunder, at least he had never plundered the poor or the helpless. And he had embraced the first chance to slip out of his rôle and back into the ways of law-abiding men. That was the great step forward. He had been able to establish himself only as a separate identity from The Red Devil because Charlie Mark, at that time, was spreading havoc in the known mask and on the famous white mare. But now that Charlie Mark no longer rode as The Red Devil, might not suspicion once again close in on him? And should his identity ever be divulged, not even the faith of Ruth Mark could withstand the shock of that revelation.

At length he fell asleep without taking off his clothes, and appeared downstairs the next morning haggard of face, only to find that Charlie Mark had outstripped him and was already on the way to the town of Hampton.

The sleep of Charlie Mark had been sound enough, saving for a single nightmare induced by the warning of Jim Curry the evening before. He dreamed that his life had ended; he stood in heaven to be judged, and one by one the witnesses against him filed past and looked him in the face—all those who had fallen under his gun in the terrible two months of his masquerade as the outlaw. One by one they went past and searched his face with eager eyes, but each was baffled. They had never seen the face beneath the mask when he killed them; they could not brand him now.

But at length a square-bearded man halted in the very act of passing, turned, and grasped the watch fob that dangled outside of his watch pocket. "It is he," said the man in the vision, and a voice asked: "Are you the man?" And in spite of his agony of resistance, Charlie Mark felt an answering voice gather in his throat and burst from his lips, damning himself with the sound of it: "Yes, I am The Red Devil."

He had wakened from this hideous nightmare wet with cold sweat; sitting up in the bed, he vowed that the first act of the next day should be to get rid of the wretched fob. Accordingly when he rose in the morning, he found the fob, stood at the window, and hurled the little bright piece of gold as far as he could fling it into the trees beyond the house.

That accomplished, he went about his dressing with an easier conscience until, going down-stairs a little later, he thought that fob might well be found under the trees at the next plowing, and that then it would be instantly recalled that he had worn it. It would be doubly suspicious if the little trinket were found in that manner. People would instantly suspect him of wishing to get rid of it for guilty reasons.

Accordingly he hurried out under the trees.

There followed an anxious search of ten or fifteen minutes until he discovered what he wanted glimmering in the shade of a bunch of dead grass. He scooped it up eagerly, and hurried toward the barn to get a shovel to bury it, but he stopped halfway there.

People were already astir in the big house and in the bunkhouse, although he had risen very early, indeed. And might he not be seen if he dug a hole? Better, far better, that he should not do so, even at night, for there would be traces of such digging. So far as he could remember, there were many tales of cunningly buried treasure, but there was never a tale in which it was not discovered in the end. Always it rejoiced the discoverer and brought endless shame and guilt upon the man who had buried the treasure, if that man were alive. Of course, there was only a small similarity between a treasure and a single watch fob, but the similarity was great enough to make it weigh heavily on the mind and the soul of the guilty youth.

He must not bury it; he must not even hide it. It was impossible to hide things, even in the broad desert. Then, if he did not hide it, would it not be well boldly and frankly to avow his ownership of the trinket in some such way as would establish his innocence?

The moment the idea came to him he welcomed it, so to speak, with open arms. That was the very thing he must do. Regardless of the early hour, feverishly eager to have this matter accomplished, he went to the barn and saddled the first horse he found in a stall and spurred toward Hampton.

The window of Josiah Watkins's loan office and pawnshop had not greatly changed since Charlie last saw it. Neither had Josiah. He was just in the act of opening his office for the day, shoving into the window tray after tray of cheap trinkets and jewelry, a very small portion of which was real. When Charlie Mark entered, the withered little proprietor tucked under the pit of his arm the feather duster with which he had been raising a cloud, and bent his head so that he could view Charlie over his glasses.

"My, my," he said. "You sure been hurrying."

"Hurrying? Not at all," said Charlie, for this idea of hurry by no means fitted in with his plans. "I've just dropped into town to see some of my friends. I let the horse have his way . . . that's all."

"*Hmm*," muttered Watkins. "Well, it sure flatters me, Charlie, to have you put me one of the first on the list."

There was such a mixture of dry sarcasm and buried humor in this remark that Charlie looked coldly on the little old man, and then produced his wallet without a direct answer.

From the wallet he drew out the fob.

"I picked this up on the road the other day," he said. "Somebody dropped it, and somebody may miss it. I thought I'd leave it here. Do you mind? The owner may happen by and claim it."

"Sure," Watkins said with a nod, "you can leave it here. But where do I come in? Maybe I spend my time here for nothing? Or maybe the room in that window ain't worth nothing at all?"

Charlie Mark smiled. "All right," he said. "I'll pay you for your space and your time. How'll a dollar do?"

"Fair to middling," said Watkins without enthusiasm. "Although it plumb mixes things up for me to start a lost and found bureau this way. But gimme the fob and a dollar. I'll put a sign up in the window. But say, how am I to know who the owner is when he comes in and claims it? Shall I tell him to go out and talk to you?"

"Talk to me?" exclaimed Charlie Mark. "I should say not. Why . . . why should I waste time on every stranger who comes along and thinks he can talk me into believing that he is the owner of the fob?"

"Well," said Watkins, "how'm I to tell?"

Into the mind of Charlie Mark flashed the face of the man who had died wearing this fob, and from whose watch it had been cut. It was a square-bearded handsome face, heavily covered with whiskers save for patches beneath the eyes where the skin showed a deep brown. This was the man who had died. But might not some friend of his know the trinket?

"Use your judgment," he said hastily.

"Where'll I say you found it?"

"Why, out on the road."

"Near your pa's place?"

Charlie was hurrying toward the door. The last thing he wanted was to be plied with questions about the finding of this infernal watch fob.

"Yes . . . that was it . . . I believe," he stammered as he backed through the door. "Do as you please about it, Watkins. I don't want to be bothered with it."

In his heart of hearts he profoundly hoped that Watkins would appropriate the fob for his own use. But little did he know the pawnbroker. The old man juggled the piece of gold for a moment in his hand, and then emitted a long, low whistle that might have meant any one of a number of things. Then he made out a large card—a card strangely large for one who valued the space in his window so highly. A moment later the curious could read as follows: **Found! Nugget watch fob. Owner make claim!**

He was so interested that he even went outside of his shop and viewed the advertisement from the street; as though he were pleased by what he saw, he went back into his shop rubbing his withered old hands.

VI

That was the beginning of two weeks and more of trouble for Josiah Watkins, familiarly known in Hampton as either Jo or Josh according to the humor of the friend who addressed him. Never in his life had he displayed in his window an attraction that called forth so much notice as the fob.

But then, never before had he made such a display. Men approached the window with sparkling eyes, expecting to find at least a few diamonds set into the fob, but they were astonished and disappointed to find that it was plain gold, and almost invariably they would go inside the shop and ask Josiah about it.

How did it come there? How could the owner prove his identity to the satisfaction of Josh?

"Leave that to me," Watkins would answer rather loftily. "I can tell when a gent's talking honest by instinct. I ain't no fence, and I've saved myself from taking stolen goods by knowing the gents that I deal with. And when the right man comes along, I'll be able to tell him."

Of course, more than once men came in and claimed the trinket.

"That looks considerable like a fob that I had

a couple of years back," they would say. "Lemme have another look at it, will you?"

"Sure," the pawnbroker would answer with unfailing good humor. "All you got to do is to tell me if they's any initials scratched on the side of it that's turned to the card just now."

No one was able to answer that small but important question until, on a morning some sixteen days after Charlie Mark brought the fob into the shop, there appeared in the doorway a man of middle height and of more than average girth of shoulder and chest. His face was densely covered with a beard that began close to the eyes and flowed down to a square-trimmed end. He advanced to the glass counter behind which Josiah Watkins officiated, and slapped his brown hand on the case.

"I've come to take a look at that fob out there in the window," he said. "Lemme see it, will you?"

"Sure," said Josiah wearily, for he had been exhausted in patience. "You can see it just as soon as you'll tell me what's on the side of it that's turned to the card."

"What d'you mean?" asked the other. "You think I'm trying to beat you out of that measly fob? Listen to me, partner. I'm Bill Ross of Crooked Creek, and anybody from that part of the country will tell you that I don't have to go around swiping measly little fobs like that. But

I'll tell you this . . . if you're asking about initials, the initials that ought to be on that fob are F R, after my brother, Frank Ross."

The pawnbroker had lifted his head and turned around full of interest at this narrative, but now his eyes darkened, and he shook his head. After all, this must be a far more aggressive claimant than the others had been, but beyond his aggressiveness he showed not the slightest proof that the fob was his or his brother's.

"Maybe you're Bill Ross," he said dryly, "and maybe Frank Ross is your brother . . . and maybe he ain't. But, anyway, if there are initials on that fob, they ain't F R. That's final. You go hunting your brother's fob some other place."

The answer, however, was not the flush of shame or the brazen laugh with which most of the claimants had met their downfall at the hands of the sturdy little Watkins. Instead, Bill Ross flushed to his black eyes, and a branching vein stood out in the center of his forehead, so great was his anger.

"I'm here to stay," he said. "You can lay to it that I take root right here till I get a look at that fob. Maybe the initials have been rubbed off, but I know that fob . . . and it used to belong to my brother."

"All right, said the pawnbroker. "Just loosen up and tell me some of the other marks that let you recognize it."

"By the hammer marks, for one thing," answered Ross. "I hammered that fob out my own self. And I can tell it by the way the ring is made on top for the strap to go through. I ain't any expert, but that was a smooth job . . . for me . . . and I remember it."

Josiah Watkins rubbed his knuckles across his chin, and the stubble of a two-day's beard rasped under the friction. There was a most convincing air to this claimant, he was forced to admit.

"That's talking pretty strong," he said. "But . . . well, when did your brother lose that fob?"

"Six weeks ago come tomorrow. No, seven weeks."

Watkins shook his head. That could hardly be correct, if it related to the fob that young Charlie Mark had found and brought in. But his patience continued to last with the conversation, for there had been something extremely suspicious in the manner of Charlie Mark when he brought that fob to be shown in the window. Charlie was not in the habit of rising early to ride clear to town to execute such missions, and old Watkins had learned by careful inquiry, later, that no sooner was the fob disposed of than Charlie Mark turned his horse and rode back for the ranch of his adopted father as fast as he had ridden toward town.

"Seven weeks," repeated Watkins, drumming

on the top of the glass case and examining Ross with eager eyes. "And where did he lose it?"

"Over in Amazon Pass."

"Amazon Pass?" Watkins shook his head. Had not Charlie Mark picked this fob up—or said he picked it up—on the road near his house?

"Why, you old idiot," roared Ross, his face turning purple in a passion of anger, "don't you suppose I'd ought to know? Wasn't that the place where my brother was killed by that murderer, The Red Devil, and didn't The Red Devil cut the fob off the strap that held it?"

"The Red Devil . . . you're sure?"

"Sure? Didn't I have to stand by with my gun on the ground and my hands in the air? Didn't I have to stand by and see it done . . . see poor Frank go down, and see that devil lean over him and slash the fob away? Oh, cuss him. I know one thing, and that is that I'm going to live long enough to get back at him!"

His whole stout body shook with the passion of this statement, and then he held out his calloused palm.

"Gimme that fob. It might talk to me about The Red Devil and where to find him."

"I'll show you," said Watkins, overawed in spite of himself by this display of emotion. "I'll let you see for yourself. The initials can't never be made into any F R."

He took the card from the window, removed

the fob, and exposed the hitherto hidden side to the eyes of Ross.

The latter exclaimed in surprise and impatience, for the two deeply cut initials were most legibly engraved **E.B.** But suddenly he snatched the fob and cried out fiercely.

"Don't run with that fob!" cried Watkins in warning. "I'll raise the town first. You ain't proved to my satisfaction that it belongs to you by rights. And you ain't going to have more'n a look at it till you do prove what I'm waiting here to hear."

"But I'm going to prove it. Look there . . . and there! Wasn't that an F to begin with, and wasn't it made into an E by cutting another line? Look close, and you'll see that the lowest line wasn't cut with the same sort of thing that was used to cut the other lines. And look at the bottom of the B, too. It was made like the lowest line of the E. The F and the R were cut in, and the other lines are stamped in, maybe with the end of a chisel, just the thing that a miner like Frank would be apt to use. D'you see? I tell you that used to read F R, but it's been changed into E B. Can't you see?"

Josiah Watkins, the color flooding out of his face, leaned low over the case, and stared as bidden. At length he took his trusty little microscope and with it continued the examination. There was no room for doubt. Different instruments had been used in the making of both letters.

He raised a wan and staring face.

"Next thing," said Ross, trembling in excitement, "is who brung this here?"

"Partner," said the pawnbroker, "I wish strongly that I never seen that fob. I thought from the first that they was something queer about him bringing it in the way he done, but I never dreamed . . . and it can't be . . . ."

"Gimme his name," pleaded the miner. "That's all I ask."

"You know it. Everybody in these parts knows it. His name is Charlie Mark."

It was a stunning blow to Bill Ross.

"Why, Watkins," he said, "I ain't accusing the gent that brung this fob here of having . . . having killed poor Frank. I ain't such a fool that I'd accuse young Mark of being The Red Devil. But I sure am going out to ask him some questions."

"If he'll answer 'em. He's proud as an eagle."

"And I'm a bit prouder and a bit wilder right now. He'll answer, right enough. You don't have to worry none about that."

He left the pawnshop with a rush and vaulted on to the saddled horse that stood with downward drowsing head in the street before the shop.

"He means business," muttered the gaping pawnbroker, and he repeated as the miner leaned over the pommel, scooped up the reins, and drove home the spurs: "He means business. I wouldn't be none surprised if this wound up in a gun play of some kind or another. Something like that is due in Hampton . . . just about due."

VII

Bill Ross had dropped the golden fob into the breast pocket of his shirt. It seemed as though the precious metal burned through to his heart and filled his veins with fire of hatred. He was on the trail of the murderer at last, he felt. And in his soul there was a wild prophecy of success. He would find The Red Devil, the murderer who all other men had failed to find in spite of their every effort.

So hotly did he spur out that dusty road that his horse was foaming from even that short distance when Bill Ross reached the Mark Ranch, flung himself from the saddle, and marched up the steps of the verandah. He saw before him a cheerful family group, so it seemed. There sat the white-headed Henry Mark, a man known far and wide through the mountains, whether in lumber camps, cow camps, or mines. Near him was a pretty-faced girl that must be his daughter. Beside her was a lounging youth dressed with over-much care to be a Westerner. That, if reports spoke true, must be the foppish Charlie Mark.

Facing this family group, there was a man still hot from riding and dusty from the range—a brown faced, handsome youth with features so strongly cut that in profile he seemed a man of thirty or some years more, and in full face he was seen to be only twenty-five. He was in the midst of a narrative of some sort connected with the range, perhaps, when the approach of Ross made him turn.

"Folks," said Bill Ross, removing his hat to the girl, "I sure hate to walk in on you this way, but I got important business. My name's Bill Ross."

The old man rose. He remembered the name, he said. He was glad to meet Bill again, and, in the meantime, these were friends he must know. One by one the introductions were completed, and Bill Ross returned to the matter in hand, looking squarely into the face of Charlie Mark.

"Gents," said Bill, "and lady, I got something to talk about that maybe you've seen before. That's this." And he exposed to them suddenly, in the palm of his hand, the golden fob.

His own eyes, however, did not remain fixed on the fob. They swept the circle of faces, and he saw Charlie Mark stiffen, and start, and then the glance of the youth flashed up and burned against his face for a keen moment.

Bill Ross blinked and stepped back a half pace. There was such suspicion, defiance, and shrewdness combined in that fiery glance that he dared not once accept all that was hinted in it.

A small voice cut through: "That's the fob that Charlie wore when he come back. Ain't it, Jim?"

Little Billy rose from nowhere and leaned on the back of Jim's chair.

"Maybe. I dunno. Looks tolerable like a lot of other fobs that I've seen," said Jim Curry negligently. "What about it, partner?"

The careless voice—the very careless voice—in connection with the rather dramatic manner in which Bill had displayed the fob, made Ross turn a frowning glance toward Curry, and he was met by a glance that was equally frowning, equally indifferent. A sudden thrill of thankfulness ran through Bill Ross that this was not the man with whom he was to have his dealings in the matter of the fob.

"I'll tell you what about it," said Bill Ross. "This here fob . . . I hear from Jo Watkins in town . . . was brung in a couple of weeks ago by Charlie Mark. Well, gents, the last time I seen it was on the watch of my brother, Frank Ross, when he was killed by The Red Devil up in Amazon Pass."

Again he searched them, to see if anyone winced. It was not that he expected to find the criminal among them—but perhaps, who could tell?—there are strange ways of picking up clues. But this time Charlie Mark merely yawned.

"This sounds a little stagey to me," he asserted. "What does it all lead to?"

"Hush, Charlie!" exclaimed Ruth Mark. "Can you speak to him in that way when his brother . . . ?"

She stopped, the large, bright-eyed glance of Bill Ross rested upon her for a grateful and appreciative moment, then it returned to Charlie Mark as he pocketed the fob.

"I'd like to know," he said, "where you found this fob."

"In the road," said Charlie.

And in his guilty heart he turned back and forth the question: was this the beginning of the end? Had not his premonition of danger, growing out of this fob, been justified? Here it was staring him in the face, practically accusing him. He must fence this man from the trail at once.

"What road?" asked Bill Ross.

"Look here!" exclaimed Charlie Mark aggressively. "What d'you mean by cornering me with questions like this? D'you think I'm The Red Devil?"

He leaned forward in his chair with a fighting light in his face. And Bill Ross was doubly amazed to see that the youngster apparently would prefer a battle to a continuation of the cross-examination. It only made his heart beat faster with the assurance that he had indeed come on the trail that led, however slowly, toward the truth to that detestable murder in the hold-up of the stage in Amazon Pass.

"I ain't a fool," said Bill Ross. "Of course, I don't think you're The Red Devil. But I'm trying to get at all you know about this fob. It may help us all to locate The Red Devil himself, and heaven knows the whole range wants that done bad enough."

"I don't like the way you go about it," said Charlie Mark sullenly. "I don't like your tone or your way of putting your questions. Try to speak like a man of breeding even if. . . ."

"Charlie!" exclaimed Henry Mark, amazed. And he turned in his chair and regarded his adopted son with blank surprise.

"He's trying to rile me, Mister Mark," said Bill Ross, crimson to the eyes, "but he ain't going to succeed. I'm here to stay until I find out what I can."

"Answer him, Charlie," commanded Henry Mark sternly, sitting up very straight in his chair. "Answer every question he puts to you. By heavens, Charlie, I'm surprised and ashamed to hear you speak as you have done."

The jaw muscles of Charlie Mark bulged, and a little spot of passion appeared momentarily in the center of his cheeks.

"What road did you find it on?" repeated the questioner.

"This road."

"When?"

"When I was coming home."

Perspiration was pouring out from every inch of his body. He was only hoping that his face did not show his emotion too much.

"When you were coming home?" echoed Ross. "When was that?"

"A couple of weeks ago."

"I want the exact day."

"Well, two weeks ago last Saturday."

"And you found the fob?"

"Yes. I've said that already."

"Between here and Hampton?"

"I think so. Yes."

"Why, Charlie," broke in Little Billy, "ain't it sort of funny that you could find a thing as little as that in the dark?"

Crimson swept at one leap over the entire face of Charlie Mark. "It was light when I saw it," he managed to gasp out. And then he became conscious that every pair of eyes was fixed upon him with a horrible earnestness.

"It couldn't have been light," said the remorseless Little Billy. "It was a long pile after dark when you come sneaking up and . . . ."

"You little snake!" growled Charlie Mark, and the back of his hard knuckles cracked across the mouth of the boy.

Little Billy reeled back against the wall of the house, and the next moment the hand of Charlie Mark was caught in a grip as of iron. He found himself inches away from the convulsed face of Jim Curry. For a moment he glared into that face whose lips were trembling over unspoken words, but Curry managed by a vast effort to control his fury, fling away the hand of Charlie, and go to Little Billy. The boy, white-faced but unflinching, gripped his hand and flashed up to him a single glance of admiration and trust. That was all.

Ruth Mark and her father were by this time on their feet. Only Charlie Mark himself was sitting. And it seemed to him that, by that brutal blow, he had betrayed himself utterly. He made a greater effort of mind than he had ever made in his life; that effort was a grip of the will to keep himself from bolting from the verandah and seeking refuge in flight.

"It was light when I started out from Hampton," he said "and, when I was walking along, I kicked this fob out of the dust. I sat down to look it over. And . . . and . . . while I was there resting, it got dark. And there you are with your infernal mystery. Is that enough talk to suit you?"

"Not quite," snapped Bill Ross.

The brain of Charlie Mark spun literally through a maze of darkness. What trap could be forthcoming now?

"What initials were on that fob?"

Frantically Charlie Mark thrust his thoughts back into the past. What were the cursed initials on the thing? E.B.? Or F.R.? An instant of reflection would have told him what was the original and what was the pair of initials to which he himself had altered it.

"The initials," he said, "were F-R."

And then he shut his teeth suddenly, seeing the eyes of Bill Ross grow wide. And he remembered. F.R. was the pair which he had changed. E.B. was what he should have said. He could see Bill Ross gaping, white with excitement and horror.

And then Ross spoke. "That's enough, I guess . . . I dunno . . . . My head's spinning. I can't believe what I've heard. But you"—and here a sudden thrill came into his voice—"you, Charlie Mark, know something about The Red Devil. You've seen him . . . you've been with him . . . because you got this fob out of his own hands, and he told you what initials was on it before he changed them himself."

VIII

It was fate, indeed, thought Charlie Mark as he lifted his guilty eyes to the stern face of Bill Ross. One important fact filtered into his dazed brain—and that was that he had not been directly accused of being The Red Devil in person—only it was insinuated that he was in some manner connected with the terrible bandit. The accusation was almost as severe. To meet it he should summon an appearance of righteous indignation as strong as possible. And he made the effort with all his heart, but the appearance of indignation would not come. Something had dissolved in him—something that should have hardened and made it possible for him to laugh defiantly. And it seemed to Charlie Mark that the weakening influence proceeded from the keenly watching eyes of Little Billy, whose face had turned so pale with excitement that his freckles stood out as great dark stains. The boy looked through and through him, and saw into every shadowy corner of his soul.

A trembling hand fell on Charlie's shoulder, and he looked up into the drawn face of Henry Mark.

"Son," the old man was saying, "get up and tell him he lies. Get up and tell him he lies before I have to do it."

Charlie Mark rubbed his knuckles across his forehead as though he wished to brush away the numbness from his brain. The mere exercise of his voice snapped the bond that held him. He leaped to his feet.

"You confounded interloper, you . . . you . . . . Get out before I throw you out. Start moving while you still can move!"

Bill Ross backed down the steps, scowling heavily. But the man he faced was not Charlie

Mark. He was watching the stern face of Jim Curry standing to one side. There, he sensed, was the gravest danger.

"I'll vamoose now," he said slowly. "I can't stand up against odds like these here ones. But if you gents think that I'm leaving this trail now, you're plumb crazy. I'm after you, Charlie Mark. If you've had dealings with The Red Devil once, you'll have dealings with him again. And I'm going to get you and follow you on the trail to meet him. Lay your money on that."

He climbed into his saddle, then turned and faced them once more.

"The minute I seen the fob," he said, "I'd knowed that I'd strike something behind it. And I have! Good bye, gents. Lady, I'm plumb sorry that I've had to come out here and make all of this excitement."

He removed his hat, bowed to the group, and then was gone down the road at a rocking lope.

Charlie Mark instantly became the center of attention. All heads turned suddenly upon him. And he, in turn, attempted to meet them with a laugh, but the sound died in his throat. He did the worst thing he could possibly have done by turning on his heel and retreating through the front door into the house, and there they heard him stamping up the stairs one by one.

Not a sound came from the wretched group on the verandah until the last of those climbing footfalls died out and the door slammed heavily from the second story of the house. Then Henry Mark, his lips parted, his face fallen into sagging lines of weakness, caught Jim Curry by the shoulder.

"Jim," he gasped out, "what does it mean?"

"I dunno," said Jim. Then he saw the eye of the girl fixed upon him in pleading, and he went on: "It's just that Charlie is mad because we didn't back him up right away. That's why he's gone inside. He's sulking like a kid, and he won't talk, simply because he knows we expect him to make some explanations. He'll sit up there in his room until one of us goes and makes up to him."

"Do you think that's it?" breathed the old man. "Do you think that's it?"

He hung on the reply of Jim. Ever since Jim has been given the place as foreman on the ranch a couple of weeks before, and in that capacity had demonstrated his worth both in handling the men and the cattle, his word had meant a great deal to the aging rancher.

"Of course that's it," said Jim, watching the face of the girl. "You go up, and you'll find him in a grouch."

"I'll go," answered Henry Mark. "Just for a minute, Jim, my heart pretty near stopped, because I thought that . . . that . . . heaven knows what. I didn't suspect Charlie, of course. But I

259

was afraid . . . young men do fool things now and then . . . and maybe. . . ."

He blundered through the front door, and they heard his hurrying but irregular step go up the stairs.

Jim Curry turned and confronted the white face of the girl. But it was Little Billy who spoke.

"Well," he said, "when I get growed up, I'm going to practice a pile . . . but I know right now that I'll never get as good at lying as you are, Jim."

"Get out!" snapped Jim Curry. "You hear too much and you see too much and you talk too much for a kid your size. Go on, now."

The half-serious and half-jesting threat of his raised hand sent Little Billy scampering off the porch. It left Jim and Ruth Mark together.

"Do you think . . . ?" she began.

"I don't think," said Jim. "Today I've laid off thinking. I'm leaving it to wiser folks than me. Just now I'm busy wondering what's going on inside of your head."

"The same thing, I imagine, that's going in inside of yours."

"Well?"

"That there's something in what Mister Ross said."

"'Eh?" exclaimed Jim. "You think that?"

The girl came close to him, her color changing under the stress of her emotion. "I don't like

Charlie," she said. "You know that. But you don't know still more . . . that I actually hate him. I've never known anything good about him. Even when he was a little youngster, he was the cruelest, cleverest, most sneaking chap in the whole countryside. I haven't changed my opinion about him in the meantime. He's gone from bad to worse. He covers his trail much better than he once did. But under the surface he's just the same Charlie Mark . . . vindictive, selfish, mean. I . . . I never have trusted him. I don't trust him now. And . . . and I think that perhaps Mister Ross may be right. Charlie may have had dealings with The Red Devil."

"You think he's as bad as that?"

"I do."

"But then maybe all we hear about The Red Devil isn't true. I've heard of outlaws who were not near as bad as their reputation. Haven't you?"

"Perhaps some of them aren't. But not The Red Devil. Why, he's proverbial."

Jim Curry bent his head a little. His plea had been for himself more than for Charlie Mark. He saw now how completely the mind of the girl was made up. Once she should connect him with his true past—once she should identify him as the man who had made the name and fame of The Red Devil so terrible throughout the mountains—then her liking for him, which was, he

261

felt, rapidly warming into something more than liking, would be destroyed. Not only would it be destroyed, but in its place there would be substituted the same aversion with which she looked on her foster brother.

"But what I wanted to talk to you about," said the girl, "is not what Charlie may be. I've known a good deal about him for a long time. What I want to do and want to get you to promise to help me in is to keep Father from finding out the truth."

It was a request that shocked Jim Curry.

"You see," explained the girl, "I expect to have a hard time to persuade you. I know that you hate Charlie even more than I hate him."

"You're sure? But, Ruth, he's. . . ."

"Never done anything to you? That doesn't matter. You hate him. Don't deny it. I've seen it in your face. I've seen it in his face. You hate him and despise him. And he hates you and fears you. Why if another man had gripped his wrist as you did when he struck Little Billy . . . the coward! . . . a moment ago, Charlie would have drawn a gun. But he was afraid to try a weapon against you. He fears you . . . just why, I can't make out. I never knew him to be afraid of any-thing before."

"All right," said Jim, "you've made out that I hate him. I won't argue. All I'll say is to ask you why you want to save him from your father."

"Because," said the girl thoughtfully, "I think Father is too old to stand the shock of the truth. Did you see him just now when Mister Ross accused Charlie, and Charlie's eyes began to glance from side to side like the eyes of a cornered rat? Well, I was hoping that Father would show a flash of suspicion and anger. I watched him closely, but all I saw in his face was horror and fear. No . . . he's accepted Charlie as a member of the family so long that I think he's almost forgotten that Charlie isn't his own son. And Charlie has grown into his heart for so long that I think it would kill him to have Charlie uprooted and taken out now. And I want you to promise that you'll do what you can to keep Father from finding out the truth . . . if that truth is what I think it must be."

Jim Curry bowed his head. It was a great deal to ask, a great deal more than the girl could dream that she was asking. It was, in a way, asking him to sign away his own hopes of her. And he signed then. He raised his head with a sigh.

"I'll do it," he said. "But listen to that. The snake has doubled back into safety again and got Mister Mark's good opinion."

A door was thrown open upstairs. Two hearty voices rolled out to them, laughing together.

"Can you beat that?" asked Jim Curry in disgust.

"No," admitted the girl.

They turned and went slowly into the house, and no sooner were they gone than the head of Little Billy popped around the corner of the verandah and watched them depart. He had lain in covert, still as a frightened rabbit, and heard the entire conversation.

"If this keeps on," said Little Billy, "I sure got to take a hand myself."

IX

A way out of the difficulty came slowly to the mind of Charlie Mark that night, and in the morning he put it into execution. He mounted his horse and rode into the little town of Hampton again, cursing that former day when he had mounted the same horse and gone in to advertise the fob in the pawnshop. Who could have thought that the fob would not be picked up by someone who had not the slightest claim to it, but who could find a way around Josiah Watkins by dint of cunning lies? Yet even if it were found by one who had known the owner, how could guilt be brought down upon his head? The impossible had happened, and in spite of everything the guilt had descended upon his head— not in the eyes of the public, perhaps, but in his own.

It seemed to Charlie Mark that there was only one way in which to avoid further danger. And he took that way.

He went to the hotel the moment he was in Hampton, and in the hotel he strode to the lobby and looked about him. It was a most prosperous and up-to-date hotel, and was the only town within a radius of fifty miles that could boast such a public room as this. There he saw at once what he wanted. Bill Ross sat in a corner brooding over a wrinkled and much-worn daily paper.

Charlie Mark stepped across the room and took an adjoining chair. He said, as Bill looked up: "Thought I'd drop in to see you, Ross. I wanted to talk things over with you, and show you that I mean to be friendly and make all the first steps to getting over our little difficulty of yesterday."

He said this in a loud voice that carried to half a dozen of the bystanders, even causing them to look carefully at Charlie Mark. He was not in the habit of showing such extreme friendliness to men of the neighborhood. But before the startled look had entirely died out of the eyes of Bill Ross as he recognized his companion, Charlie Mark continued in a voice pitched so low that only Bill could hear: "That's for the blockheads hanging around. And what I mean is blow your fool head off."

Bill Ross had turned gray, but his eyes did not falter.

"Well, son," he said in a voice as level and as controlled as that of Charlie Mark, "ain't you making a good deal of a fool of yourself to go around saying things like that? Can't I just call the notice of folks to you?"

"But you won't," said Charlie Mark. "I know your kind. You're going to stay right here and let me finish my talk."

"How d'you figure that?"

"Because, Bill, there's one thing you're more afraid of than you're afraid of death, and that is of losing your reputation as a brave man. Am I right? You wouldn't whine and call for help if any one man in the world jumped you . . . not even The Red Devil."

"Maybe not," said Bill Ross steadily. "I ain't showed the white feather yet, and I figure that I'll get along for a time still without showing it. You're right that far, kid. I ain't going to holler for help . . . not if ten the like of you should jump me."

The sneer froze on the lips of Charlie Mark. "Aren't you?" he said. "Listen to me, my friend. I'm going to make you sweat for a minute or two. Do you know me?"

"I know you for a promising young scoundrel, if my suspicions are right." said Bill Ross. "And my suspicions, Charlie Mark, are that you've been playing hand in glove with The Red Devil. He's needed ways of keeping in touch with men. He's needed some place where he could collect information. Why couldn't you be the man? You're a free spender. Where do you get the money? In fact, Charlie Mark, I think I'm going to make you do the sweating."

Charlie Mark chuckled softly. "You fool!" he said. "You thick-headed idiot . . . I'm The Red Devil myself." Adding, as Bill Ross drew back blinking: "I'm not joking. I mean it."

"You mean you'd come to me and put your neck in a noose?"

"Not a bit. Try it. Stand up and get on your legs and tell the folks here that I'm The Red Devil because I've just told you so. What will they do? They'll put you in an asylum and never let the crazy man out."

"And they'd have a right to keep me there if I'd believe such a crazy yarn as that. You mean for six years you have . . . ?"

"Not six. Suppose that I met The Red Devil and that he and I had a talk and I finally wound up by stepping into the shoes of the bandit? Think of that, Bill."

"You're crazy."

"I'll prove to you in a minute that I'm not. What was in your brother's wallet when he died?"

"Money in bills," said Ross, fascinated by this

new and terrible turn to the conversation that was still carried out in careful murmurs.

"And what else?"

Ross shivered. "Do you know?"

"A picture of the family."

"The Red Devil told you," muttered Ross, moistening his colorless lips.

"Bah!" sneered Charlie Mark. "I'll prove it another way. Here's something The Red Devil wouldn't have been apt to tell me even if he and I were as thick as you seem to think we must be. Here's something that only you and I would have been apt to know and notice and remember. When you threw your revolver on the ground at my command, the butt pointed to me and the muzzle at you."

The last vestige of color left the face of Bill Ross.

"Are you the devil?" he gasped out.

"The Red Devil," said Charlie.

"By heaven, I think . . . ."

"Hush," said Charlie Mark. "Utter one whisper of what you think, and they'll arrest you for a madman."

"It's not I that is mad," said Bill Ross. "It's you . . . it's you that are mad for telling me this."

"You think that I have no reason for talking to you as I have been doing?"

"No sane reason."

"Wrong . . . all wrong. Bill, I had to tell you this

to kill your nerve. You're a steady man with a gun. I could tell that by one look at you. And though I've been known to take chances, I don't wish to if I can avoid it. I'm not taking chances now. I've told you what I am and you're done, Bill. Your color's gone, and your hand shakes. You're sick inside, and you look sick on the outside. I almost pity you."

In fact, the honest-hearted miner was white and trembling, although still he was able to keep his eye fixed on the sneering face of Charlie Mark.

"Pity be hanged," breathed Bill. "There ain't enough bullets in the world to kill me before I get you."

"Hush," warned Charlie Mark. "They've heard you say that. They've heard your tone at least. And now the people around here will think that you are the aggressor."

"Eh?"

"I'm going to stand up, Bill, and smash you across the mouth with my left hand . . . ."

"You coyote."

"And when you pull your gun, I'm going to draw my own Colt with my right hand and fill you full of lead. Understand?"

"You can't bluff me," said Bill Ross. But the sweat was streaming down his face.

"Can't I? Just watch. You have to go for your gat . . . you don't dare take water from me. That'd be worse than death. You'll go for your gun, but your nerve is gone now, and you wouldn't hit the side of a barn. You're no better'n dead, Bill Ross."

"You *are* The Red Devil."

"Aye, and that's why I have to kill you. You know too much."

"You . . . you . . . ."

"No words bad enough for me? Perhaps not. But not a hand will touch me for killing you. A dozen men will swear that they heard me come in and tell you that I'd come in to smooth things up. A dozen men will say that, as we talked together, you began to raise your voice and swear, while I kept cool until at last I was insulted, jumped to my feet, and slapped you. Then you drew your gun or made a pass for it . . . and I killed you before the gat was out of its leather. Does that seem clear to you, Ross?"

"You can't do it," said Ross.

"Watch."

With that word he sprang up. Bill Ross folded his arms.

"You can't say that to me!" cried Charlie Mark so that every head in the room was turned toward him. "You can't say that. I'll take that from no man. Even if I don't know the name of my father, nobody can accuse . . . ."

And to complete the sentence, he whipped his open hand across the mouth of Bill Ross so that the sound was like the smacking together of two palms.

At the same instant he went for his gun and brought it out with a marvelously dexterous flip. But he did not shoot. And the muscles of the other men in the room, drawn taut to meet the sound of the exploding gun, gradually relaxed. Bill Ross had not gone for his own weapon.

With arms still folded, sitting erect in his chair, he allowed a crimson flush to mount his face and to bring out in bold relief the white print where Charlie Mark's fingers had struck; still he did not stir. When he did move, it was to rise slowly, very slowly, and face the little crowd, a crowd horror-stricken at the sight of a man who had once been brave but who now, in public, had taken water.

The faces that watched Bill Ross were sick with disgust and horror.

"Gents," said Bill Ross, "I got to ask you to give me a chance. Some of you have heard of me. And you've never heard of me playing yaller yet. And sooner or later I'll show you why I had to show the white feather today. The yarn is too long for telling. And it wouldn't be believed when it was told. But someday, so help me heaven, I'll hang Charlie Mark higher than the ceiling of this room . . . and, when he hangs, it will be the public hangman that does the work."

There was something so solemn and so delib-
erate in this denunciation that the disgust
vanished from the faces of his listeners, and
astonishment took its place. Bill Ross walked
slowly out of the room. A deathly silence was left
behind him, only slowly broken as whispers
began here and there, and someone murmured:
"Look at Charlie Mark."

His face was worth long and careful observation. Conscious that he had played too many
cards, and that he had not only showed his hand
but also lost the game, had convulsed his naturally handsome features and made his com-
plexion livid. For a long moment he remained
staring down at the chair as though the broad
form of Bill Ross were still ensconced in it.
Then he thrust his drawn revolver back into its
holster, and, with a dark scowl on those who
stood about the room, he stalked rapidly out of it.

Instantly there was a breath of relief drawn by
every man, and a single expression burst from
their lips: "That kid will come to no good end."

X

A pleasant bass voice greeted Charlie Mark as
he passed through the door. He turned sharply,
but his eyes were veiled by his passion; it was a
few seconds before he was able to recognize in

the tall bulky form of the rancher who leaned against the wall that same J.C. Butler who had so unmercifully trimmed him on the train. He was rolling a cigarette. And Charlie Mark noted, with disgust and surprise, that Butler looked as much at home in his rough outfit as he had looked on the train in civilized clothes. He was quite at ease in the simple but exacting task of rolling the cigarette, and, while he tapped the side of the smoke to jog the tobacco down in the paper, he looked with a quiet smile at Charlie Mark.

"Hello," was his greeting. "You out here playing the small time?"

Charlie Mark paused. $32,000 of his money was in the possession of that fat, amiable-looking grafter. Bill Ross was suddenly half forgotten.

"What do you mean?" asked Charlie Mark. "What do you mean by small time?"

Butler glanced around and made sure that no one was near.

"Tut, tut," he said. "I don't blame you. I'm doing it myself. Amazing amount of money around here, but not such easy work to get it out. Matter of fact, I'm a couple of thousand down just now myself. And as for you . . . well, son, you may pick up a good deal of experience on this circuit, but I'm hanged if I see how you can make traveling expenses. Are you daubing them or using the peg?"

The cant of the professional gambler flowed

smoothly from his tongue. And a great, quick-born hope kept Charlie Mark from indulging in the stream of profanity to which his instincts urged him.

"Is your partner with you?" he asked.

"Warner? He's working up a little stuff for me down the road. He's working light, though. I carry the wad. I'm the rich fall guy, you see, and he gets these rubes all fixed for plucking me. Just now I'm up here doing a little bit for myself . . . and not doing very well, as I said before. However, I've planted the little old tin can here full of green boys, and I guess I'll break even before I quit."

It was astonishing to hear the glib ease with which he gossiped with his victim. Charlie Mark gazed upon the big man with a touch of awe. Would he himself ever be able to summon such effrontery?

"What I wonder," he said, "is why you are still working. I should think you'd have retired long ago."

"I have plenty for myself, lad," said Butler. "But I need a few nest eggs to start the girls, three charming daughters. You must come and look us over one of these days."

"I hope," said Charlie Mark, with a good grace that surprised himself more than it surprised Butler, "that my thirty-two thousand will make them happy."

"One of them," corrected Mr. Butler. "It will keep Alice in automobiles this year, I hope. The dear girl has taken a fancy to fast cars, and the way she crumples them up is shameful."

"Must be," grunted Charlie Mark. "I'll see you later."

Turning his back on the old rascal, he wandered off by himself. A plan was growing rapidly to maturity in his brain. The elderly gambler had stated that his capital was sunk in the hotel tin can, or safe. That capital must be very large indeed. In order to win a great deal of money, a gambler on the scale of Butler must be prepared to lose a great deal, also, from time to time. There might be in that safe $20,000 to $30,000—or even more. Suppose, then, that a crafty yegg were to blow that safe. Would not the haul be fairly rich, with the money of other guests of the hotel included?

To be sure, he was no expert in safe-cracking, but, then, everyone had to make a start sooner of later at what they do, and this was as good a time as any to learn his first practical lesson, be revenged on Butler, and gain, at the same time, some needed recreation.

It was a dangerous job, but that added to the pleasure.

He returned to the ranch and spent the rest of the day accumulating what he needed—dynamite from which the soup was to be made, yellow laundry soap for his mold in which to run the explosive around the door of the safe, and a fuse with which to send off the charge. It required some adroit rummaging to get all that he needed, but since his father occasionally took a turn through the mountains, harking back to earlier days by doing a bit of prospecting and mild mining, Charlie was able to get what he needed.

In the early evening, just after dinner, he excused himself, saddled a horse, and jogged off with his kit of implements for the safe-cracking. No questions were asked, for it was an old trick of his to slip out into the night for no express goal and return at odd hours in the morning. He had decided upon completely horrifying and baffling the men of Hampton by leaving behind him, after the blowing of the safe, the mark by which Jim Curry, in his former days of outlawry, had been in the habit of branding his work—an open hand roughly sketched on a board with the point of a knife. Charlie Mark had practiced the trick until it was as fluently at his command as at the command of Jim Curry himself. Tonight he would use it, and thereby, for Bill Ross, identify himself as the robber.

But what could Bill Ross do? He could not bring accusations without evidence to back them up, and that evidence he would never get.

It was midnight before Charlie's fire in the slough bed had cooked the soup, and, when that

276

precious liquid had been drawn off and bottled with care, Charlie Mark gathered his materials together and made on again toward the town, cutting in from the back.

He came past the barn of Sheriff Nance, his mind going vividly back to that pleasant occasion on which he had robbed the sheriff. There he left his horse, for it was not a long distance from the barn to the hotel, and the shadow behind the barn made an excellent place to conceal his mount.

He paused again to arrange one more pleasing detail, which was to place a red wig on his head and let a handkerchief fall over his face by way of a mask. Then he hurried on toward the scene of action.

The hotel was utterly quiet. For that matter, so was the village street; folks led busy lives in Hampton, and consequently they went to bed early. There was only one lighted window, and that in the highest story of the old hotel. He, of course, could not tell who was in that room, yet he might have guessed the truth—that it was Bill Ross, kept awake by shame and the tormenting knowledge that he must find some manner of following up a clue that would reveal the murderer, the outlaw, the self-confessed bandit, to the good people of the town.

No clue or hope for a clue was revealed to the patient searcher. Hour after hour he had sat in his room with his elbows planted on the edge of the table and his face buried in his hands. And nothing occurred to him, nothing he might do to draw away the curtain and show the world the truth about Charlie Mark.

Midnight passed. 1:00 had come, and he was turning toward his bed when the hotel was shaken as though a sudden gust of wind had struck it. Instantly afterward the blow was followed by a deep, choked report.

That noise wakened the miner brain of Bill Ross, and he forgot his troubles. His hat was on his head at once, his revolver in his hand, and he plunged down the stairs to the first floor where a strange, thick, disagreeable odor greeted his nostrils.

By the wreckage he was led to the scene of the disaster. For that matter, had he been in doubt, a dozen voices and a dozen lights, which now appeared, would have led him to the place. They stumbled back through the lobby and to the little room that served as an office for the proprietor. There he stood, white of face, his fat hands pressed silently together. He was in his nightgown, the draft wagging the bottom of the garment about his red, fat knees. And as they rushed in, he merely raised his wan face toward them with eyes that seemed about to bulge out of their sockets.

"Who . . . what . . . how . . . ?"

And then a chorus of oaths made up the first

outburst of the cowpunchers who were staying overnight in the hotel, and who had turned out to examine into the cause of the disturbance.

But Bill Ross was attracted by a calm voice, saying: "I'm not surprised. I thought this might happen tonight."

And he turned and saw a tall, fleshy man a little bent with years, and with a reddish, kindly face.

"Second guessers always guess right," said Bill Ross. "But who done it?"

For answer the proprietor raised his hand and pointed toward a corner of the room. Instantly half a dozen men crowded in that direction. There, rudely carved into the wood, was the well-known and dreaded sign of The Red Devil, a hand drawn on the board.

Bill Ross leaped to the center of the room.

"Gents," he said, "I see Sheriff Nance coming. I suppose he has the job of saying where we should go, but I want to ask half a dozen of you to foller me. Will you come?"

"Lead the way," said Sheriff Nance, taking in the situation and the brand of the destroyer in a glance. "We'll all follow. Heaven help you, though, if you're playing crooked."

There was a joyous shout from Bill Ross.

"Get you hosses *pronto*, and them that start late, ride like blazes straight out for the old Mark place."

XI

This, of course, was exactly what Charlie Mark expected the pursuers to do, and he planned to beat them just far enough to enable him to reach the ranch. There he could unsaddle his own horse, turn it into a pasture where it would soon remove all sign of the ride by a roll in the dust, and then rush to the house, throw off his clothes, and present a picture of bored nonchalance when the posse arrived. He could well be sure that every member of the household would have been asleep for so long that they would not know when he had returned from his ride. But everyone could truthfully state that since his boyhood it had been his habit to take such rides —which should remove all suspicion from the minds of everyone saving Bill Ross, who knew the truth.

As for the loot from the safe, it would not be too hard to dispose of. Out of the midnight incursion the total profits of Charlie Mark were $32. Butler, shrewd old thief that he was, had talked of trusting the safe, but in reality the only steel he had confidence in was the steel of his own watchfulness. Charlie Mark writhed when he thought how easily he had been taken in.

He writhed, and then he took out some of his

anger on the horse the moment he had swung into the saddle, for he struck the little mustang with both spurs and quirt. This was very foolish, because the mustang was a Roman-nosed roan with a habit of thinking for himself. To be struck with the quirt was all a matter of course, and to be stabbed with the spurs was also a pain that he must accept in a day's work, but to receive two blows at once, to his way of thinking, was entirely too much. Consequently he burst into a fury of bucking.

Bitterly vital minutes were wasted there behind the village, minutes during which Charlie Mark heard the tumult hastening through the town before he was able to make his horse bolt away across the fields.

Would he be far enough ahead now to accomplish all the things he had said he must do? He rode the distance to the ranch house like mad, often glancing behind him, but the ups and downs of the way cut him off from a chance to watch the road for any great distance behind him. At the ranch, he snatched the saddle off the mustang, threw it into the shed, whipped the roan through the gate into the pasture, and then rushed for the house, undressing on the way.

But he was too late.

From the window of his room he saw them coming down the road like mad—a full score of men lashing their horses.

The door *clicked*. He turned and saw Jim Curry just behind him.

"Put up your gat," said Jim Curry contemptuously, for at the first light sound the weapon had leaped into the hand of Charlie Mark. "I knew you'd be up to some sort of cussedness tonight. I couldn't sleep for thinking about it."

Charlie Mark glanced wildly at the half dressed figure behind him, then turned and pointed down the road. In half a minute or very little more they would be at the house, and in that case he could not possibly get out of clothes that were redolent of fresh sweat. One glance through the window had told the story to Jim Curry.

"You fool," he said, "why did you come here?"

"The horse balked with me," muttered Charlie Mark, "and . . . ."

"And what are you going to do?"

"What can I do? I haven't time to get to the pasture and rope another horse and . . . . Lord, what will Father say? What will he do to save me . . . ?"

He was pressed back against the wall, his nerve fast leaving him, his hands shaking. That mention of the father was a blow to Jim Curry. He remembered in a flash all the long list of the rancher's kindnesses to him—all the words of Ruth concerning what might happen if the foster son were found out by the law in a criminal act—not what would happen to Charlie Mark, but to the doting old man who had adopted him.

And he saw in a flash a way of repaying the father and of obeying the girl. It was bitterly hard. It meant alienating Henry Mark forever; it meant turning the mind of the girl so that she would loathe him and the very thought of him. But after all, was it not true that he could never aspire to her hand? There was too much in his past that might someday be known.

These things darted through his brain all in the space of the half second while he stood staring at the rapidly approaching cavalcade of horsemen. He turned on Charlie Mark with a curse that was a groan.

In an instant he was in his room. To jump into trousers, hook cartridge belt over his left arm, and draw the revolver, was the act of a moment. He rushed through the hall, past the stupefied Charlie Mark, only pausing to lay a crushing grip upon his shoulder and say: "I'm giving you a chance. I'm stepping into fire . . . not for your sake, but for the sake of the old man. Charlie, brace up and in heaven's name be a man. Will you try?"

Jim waited for no answer, but plunged down the hall, dashed open a window at the far end, and climbed into it. The next instant he jumped through, and his feet *thudded* on the roof of the kitchen below.

A second more, and a shrill yell broke from the posse. Then guns exploded. Charlie Mark raced for the window and hung in it, breathless. There across the yard toward the pasture fled Jim Curry, running as he had never seen man run before. The quick eyes in the posse had instantly seen him jump—as now they were spurring hard to cut him off from the horses in the pasture, riding with their flashing guns poised to shoot.

And as Jim Curry ran, he raised his voice and sent a wild calling thrilling ahead of him: "Meg! Oh, Meg!"

The heart of Charlie Mark leaped into his throat. He hated and dreaded Jim Curry, and yet with all his soul he now prayed that the gun-fighter might escape. In fact, a silver form, thin as mist in the distant night, detached itself from among the crowd of darker horses in the pasture and swept at a gallop toward the fugitive. It was white Meg coming to the call of the master, white Meg, who in the days of his outlawry, had so often saved the life and limb of Jim Curry.

She came again, like a white flash as she gathered headway. And the posse, making out what was in danger of happening—their prey carried off from under their noses, so to speak— let loose a volley of curses and shots.

At the same time Ruth and her father came down the hall and reached Charlie's side with a rush.

"Who . . . ?" she began, and then answered her own question. "Jim is out there, and all those . . . ."

"Jim?" mocked Charlie Mark. "I tell you it's The Red Devil and making his last run, at that. They're going to get him."

"The Red Devil?" cried the girl and her father in one breath.

White Meg rose at the fence, cleared it like a bird, and the next moment Jim Curry was on her bare back and, guiding her with the pressure of his hand, had sent her racing off and over the top of a slight eminence out of view. After the rider streamed the posse, their guns *crackling* like mad as they realized that in another two minutes mare and rider, at that terrific, racing gait, would be beyond capture.

And then Charlie Mark was roused by a sound of broken-hearted weeping beside him, and looked and saw Ruth Mark staring after the pursued with the tears streaming down her cheeks; beside her was the tense, agonized face of the old man. And a sudden softening came over the heart of Charlie Mark.

The great sacrifice had been made for his sake, it seemed—not for him so much as for the girl and her father, no doubt, but, nevertheless, here was a man who was laying down his life that another man, a worthless man, might have a chance to live.

His sombrero had remained on the head of Charlie. He dragged it off instinctively and let the chill air of the night blow around his temples.

From the distance a more and increasingly scattered echo of gunshots blew back to them, and at length the noise died out. Plainly The Red Devil was loose once more, and beyond the pursuit.

Center Point Publishing
600 Brooks Road • PO Box 1
Thorndike ME 04986-0001 USA

(207) 568-3717

US & Canada:
1 800 929-9108
www.centerpointlargeprint.com

ABOUT THE AUTHOR

Max Brand is the best-known pen name of Frederick Faust, creator of Dr. Kildare, Destry, and many other fictional characters popular with readers and viewers worldwide. Faust wrote for a variety of audiences in many genres. His enormous output, totaling approximately thirty million words or the equivalent of five hundred thirty ordinary books, covered nearly every field: crime, fantasy, historical romance, espionage, Westerns, science fiction, adventure, animal stories, love, war, and fashionable society, big business and big medicine. Eighty motion pictures have been based on his work along with many radio and television programs. For good measure he also published four volumes of poetry. Perhaps no other author has reached more people in more different ways.

Born in Seattle in 1892, orphaned early, Faust grew up in the rural San Joaquin Valley of California. At Berkeley he became a student rebel and one-man literary movement, contributing prodigiously to all campus publications. Denied a degree because of unconventional conduct, he embarked on a series of adventures culminating in New York City where, after a period of near starvation, he received simultaneous recognition as a serious poet and successful author of fiction. Later, he traveled widely, making his home in New York, then in Florence, and finally in Los Angeles.

Once the United States entered the Second World War, Faust abandoned his lucrative writing career and his work as a screenwriter to serve as a war correspondent with the infantry in Italy, despite his fifty-one years and a bad heart. He was killed during a night attack on a hilltop village held by the German army. New books based on magazine serials or unpublished manuscripts or restored versions continue to appear so that, alive or dead, he has averaged a new book every four months for seventy-five years. Beyond this, some work by him is newly reprinted every week of every year in one or another format somewhere in the world. A great deal more about this author and his work can be found in THE MAX BRAND COMPANION (Greenwood Press, 1997) edited by Jon Tuska and Vicki Piekarski. His next Circle V Western will be VALLEY OF OUTLAWS. His Website is www.MaxBrandOnline.com.